DADDY'S SWEET GIRL

A DARK STEPFAMILY LOVE STORY

STASIA BLACK

Copyright © 2017 Stasia Black

ISBN 13: 978-1548902568

All rights reserved. No part of this publication may be reproduced, distributed, or transmitted in any form or by any means, including photocopying, recording, or other electronic or mechanical methods, without the prior written permission of the publisher, except in the case of brief quotations embodied in critical reviews and certain other noncommercial uses permitted by copyright law.

This is a work of fiction. Similarities to real people, places, or events are entirely coincidental.

NEWSLETTER SIGN-UP

Want to read an EXCLUSIVE, FREE novella, *Indecent: a Taboo Proposal*, that is available ONLY to my newsletter subscribers, along with news about upcoming releases, sales, exclusive giveaways, and more?

When Mia's boyfriend takes her out to her favorite restaurant on their six-year anniversary, she's expecting one kind of proposal. What she didn't expect was her boyfriend's longtime rival, Vaughn McBride, to show up and make a completely different sort of offer: all her boyfriend's debts will be wiped clear. The price?

One night with her.

Sign-up for Stasia's newsletter to grab your free copy of *Indecent*.

PLEASE VISIT: BIT.LY/INDECENTSTASIABLACK

ONE

Mom's getting married today. Again. This will be husband number three. The rehearsal dinner last night was the second time I'd met the husband-to-be, Paul, and his son.

And let me just say: I don't get it. The man is beautiful. I mean, we're talking godlike gorgeous. He's blond, has a chiseled-jaw, straight nose, and is Viking kind of handsome. He keeps his hair short and there's some gray at the edges of his temple, but he's the kind of mid-forties that women complain about—how it's not fair that men get better looking as they age.

His son is a mini-me version of him, but I barely even looked at the guy. Frankly, he's just gotta be a douchebag who screws everything that moves being that good looking at twenty-four years old, right? Plus he's a doctor. Well, a doctor in training, anyway. On his dad, the gorgeousness has had a chance to age and settle into some fabulous grooves like a fine wine. Much more attractive.

And the man is marrying my mother.

Um. What?

My mother is also in her forties. But where Mr. Winters wears his age like an aforementioned god, Mom wears it like... hmm, how shall we put this? Let's just say that my Mom's an aging beauty queen who's three plastic surgery attempts did little more than twist and pull her leathery, tanning-bed-worshipping ass into a simulacrum of a slightly melted Barbie-doll on meth?

Okay, so she doesn't do meth.

Coke is her drug of choice.

She's never been able to hold down an actual job because of it.

See what I'm talking about?

She's a real winner.

Mr. Winters is the head of an oncology department of a prestigious Boston hospital. So again, what on earth is he doing with Mommy dearest?

"What did you do to that dress?" Mom asks, coming into my dressing room at the church. I know, a church. And she's wearing *white*. The ironies of this day will never cease.

I look her up and down. She's managed to squeeze herself into a lovely Vera Wang dress—she mentioned that it was *actual Vera Wang* about ten thousand times last night. Completely ignoring the fact that she managed to get an *actual Vera Wang* because of Mr. Winter's wealth or maybe Grandpa's influence. It had nothing to do with anything *she* did. Being one of the oldest families in Boston does still come with some privileges, even if we're almost broke.

Well, not anymore that Mom's marrying Mr. Winters. He's handsome *and* wealthy.

Again. *What* is he doing with Mom?

"I just had it altered a little so it fits better." I look at Mom in the mirror.

Mom's eyes narrow. "It fit just the way it was supposed to."

My brows furrow. "But it was baggy and sagged in the stomach." Not to mention the high collar that almost choked me.

Mom looks at me like, *and?*

"So I went and got it tailored to fit."

She lets out a huff of frustration. "The point of a bridesmaid dress is to be ugly so you don't upstage the bride. God, don't you know anything? That's it," she declares, throwing her hands up in the air. "There's no way you can be my maid of honor looking like that. It's bad enough that I have a *nineteen* year old daughter." She shakes her head. "I still say you should have been the fucking flower girl. Anyway. Marla will have to take your place and you can stand at the end of the line."

I look down at the dress. "It's still not exactly..." I pause, momentarily at a loss for words, "flattering."

She chose the most unattractive shade of orange I've ever seen, sure to clash with any person's skin tone, no matter your ethnicity. I've gone as natural as possible with my makeup and worn my dark brown hair in an updo, but you just can't ignore the ugly ass frock covering my body.

Mom clucks her tongue at me. "This is my special day, Sarah Elizabeth, so don't even start with me."

I sigh and back down. "Of course, Mom. Whatever you want." The path of least resistance. I know from long experience it's the easiest way to approach conflict with Mom.

"Now, go get all the other girls together and tell Marla she's my new maid of honor. Exchange your flowers for hers and make everyone get in their places."

I head out.

Within twenty minutes, me and twelve—yes *twelve*—other bridesmaids, along with corresponding groomsmen are all corralled in the foyer of the church. Or do you call them brides-matrons at this point, considering they're all Mom's friends and most of them have been divorced at least once, some several times like Mom?

Only a couple others had the same idea I did and got the gowns altered. I mean, we all look ridiculous, but the rest of them look absolutely atrocious in the shiny orange sherbet fabric covering their bodies.

"Ready for this?" asks Dominick, my soon to be brother-in-law. He holds out his arm and flashes a brilliant smile at me, golden hair gleaming in the light pouring in from the high, stained glass window.

He wears his hair longer than his dad, in a shaggy Cali surfer dude style that sweeps down over his forehead.

Man, this guy is just too slick. I smile back at him, but you know that overused saying, a person *smiles but it doesn't reach their eyes?* Yeah, my smile is one of those kinds. Patented, pasted on, and perfectly perfunctory. The kind I always use at these kinds of engagements that I get dragged to occasionally. Mostly because of Grandpa's 'old money' name or Mom's desperation to still be included in important circles. Having a daughter that she's ostensibly chaperoning and introducing to Boston society helps cover up some of the stink of being a desperate thrice used-up trophy wife.

But here Mom is, getting to live out her glory days once again. Wife once more, even if her husband is more the trophy than her now. Especially since Mr. Winters actually has a job in addition to being so dang pretty.

The organ music starts up.

"Sorry, I'm not the maid of honor anymore." I ignore Dominick's proffered arm and point to Marla, a loud woman with hair dyed a brassy red who I suspect Mom keeps around as a *best friend* because she makes Mom look comparatively prettier and thinner. "That's the woman you're escorting now. Have fun." My smile gets a touch more genuine at the flash of dismay that crosses Dominick's face as the groomsmen line up. I head toward an older gentleman at the end of the queue.

The procession starts as soon as Mom makes an appearance a few minutes later. I walk down the aisle, surprised at how packed the church is on both sides. It's easy to think that Mom's alienated everyone who she's ever met. But when I get to the front pew and see Grandpa smiling not at Mom, but me, I remember who all these people are really here for.

Grandpa might not have the fortune he once had, but he's still a wealthy man. The fact that he cut off his daughter is a well-kept secret, though apparently Mom's husband-to-be is aware.

How do I know that little tid-bit?

Well, I *miiiiight* have taken him aside last night after he sat right beside Mom as she drank flute after flute of champagne all through dinner, his gaze nothing but benevolent as he looked fondly at her.

He excused himself to the bathroom and I followed a few minutes later.

"You know she doesn't have money?" I asked right after he came out of the bathroom. The hallway was narrow and dark, off the kitchens and not well traveled.

"Excuse me?" he asked, eyebrows arching in surprise. He stood his ground, though, and didn't brush me off.

I immediately felt like a small child despite my three-inch heels. "Um. My Mom. She doesn't— I mean…" I gulped, looking down at the floor before gathering my courage to gaze back up at the towering blond Viking god-man. He is the handsomest man I've ever. "There's no money. If that's why you're marrying her. Grandpa isn't even that rich anymore. And he cut us off anyway. So if that's why you're doing it." My whole body was trembling at this point. Oh God, I just needed to get this out and then I could go hide in the coat closet for the rest of the night. "…you shouldn't. Because you know. There's none. No m-money." And with that last stumble of words I turned on my pointy little heels and fled.

And now, here I was at the front of the church. I couldn't put it off any longer. I finally lift my eyes and there he is.

The Viking god in all his spectacular glory. His barrel chest looks barely constrained in his tuxedo.

I expect his gaze to be focused past me and on my mother. His blushing bride who's ostensibly standing at the back of the church, about to come walking down the aisle toward him.

But no. His eyes are zeroed in directly on me.

It's just for a few seconds. A moment where our gazes lock. And hold.

I'm walking down the center aisle of a church, holding flowers.

A man stands there awaiting me. A glint in his eye just for me. Or so it feels.

And then the groomsman holding my arm directs me away to the side and the connection is lost.

It takes everything in me but I don't look over my shoulder. It would be too desperate.

And *wrong*.

God, what am I doing? This is my mother's *wedding*! And I'm hoping that the groom is making eyes at me? A man twice my age. A man that my mother is *marrying*?

I squeeze my eyes shut and give my head a little shake right after I take my position at the end of the bridesmaid line. Oh my gosh, is it finally happening? I've always been terrified that I was doomed to be screwed up after my upbringing with an unstable, drunk and occasional (when she could afford it) cokehead for a mom. Not to mention an absentee dad who took off when I was five because of my aforementioned batshit Mom.

I was the one trying to balance the budget at ten years old. You know, back when we *had* money before Mom blew straight through it on blowout bashes for her and her friends in the Caribbean.

Grandpa cut us off when I was fourteen, but he made sure I was in the room for the discussion because he wasn't an idiot. And he didn't cut us off completely. He continued paying via a grocery app to deliver groceries—stuff that Mom couldn't return in order to get money for blow. I could come to him if I needed clothes. He paid for Mom to go to rehab a few times. It might stick for a month or two.

But he always stopped short of letting me come live with him. I think he was always conscious of how it would look.

Did that hurt? Sure.

But whatever.

I'm *not* screwed up by it all.

I'm surviving just fine. I'm going to a great college.

Okay, so I have to live at home and I'm in debt up to my eyeballs in school loans, but I'm not going to get mired down by all my childhood crap.

I'm rising above.

I sneak another look at my mom's new husband.

God, why does he have to be *that* good looking?

That thick corded neck leading to his wide jaw. I'm sure he must've shaved this morning, but there's just the barest hint of stubble there. His beard must come in darker than the hair on his head to make such a shadow. Come to think of it, every time I've seen him, he always has that shadow on his face. A little shudder works its way down my body at the thought. It just screams such masculinity and...virility.

My cheeks heat at the thought and all sorts of flashing images that accompany it. His broad chest and the dusting of hair that no doubt coats it. I can't help imagining him crouched over a woman, lowering his body over her. Thrusting—

I jerk my eyes away from Mr. Winters. Only for them to snag on the man standing right beside him.

Dominick.

Maybe my eyes are caught because he's looking right at me. He's just blatantly out and out staring.

The easy-going smile he had in the lobby of the church is gone. There's a different quality or...intensity, if that's the right word, to the way his lips curl up as he watches me watch him. His eyes drop down ever so slightly.

Wait, is he—

He *so* is. He's ogling my cleavage. I mean, there's not a lot of it with this dress. Or any dress, to be honest. I was flat as a board forever and only just in the last couple years finally developed small little B-cup breasts. But I was aware that the gown was for my mother's wedding, so I didn't bother wearing the push-up bra I often wear to enhance my small assets.

But Dominick just stares at my dipping neckline like it can reveal all the mysteries of the universe. Even though he's about to be *my stepbrother* for god's sake.

Like you weren't just eyeing your stepfather like a hungry ham shank?

Dominick's mouth curls up even higher.

Oh my God, what is going on? A month ago, I was doing so good at the being-a-normal-girl thing and not getting sucked into Mom's vortex of crazy. I jerk my gaze away from both Dominick and his father and stare at the floor. There. That's nice and safe.

I examine the fascinating world of carpet fibers for the rest of the wedding ceremony. And I do not, do *not* listen to my mother's cringeworthy ooey gooey vows that she wrote herself about how Mr. Winters is her true, *true* soulmate and she can't live without him.

Is that as opposed to Henry, her last husband who was only her true soulmate—with just a single 'true,' aka, not her *real* as in *for realsies for realsies* soul mate. In fact, I bet if I play back the video of that ceremony that's on the shelf somewhere, these vows Mom supposedly wrote for today will sound strikingly similar to the ones she did for that wedding. And all of it she probably copied from some wedding ceremony she saw after googling vows online.

My mom does the appearance of sincerity so well.

Gah, I do not need all of this negativity in my brain or my life. Mom is a fake. I know this. Me stewing in her hypocrisy and grossness does nothing but make me feel gross and steeped in bad juju.

But there was no way I could skip the wedding. My participation was required by all involved. I get to live rent free in Boston.

So stop with the bitching, Sarah.

I just have to whisper that to myself about fifty-three more times and *voila*, the ceremony's over. Look at that. The power of positive thinking.

Glass half full. That's totally going to be my outlook from now on. And if all else fails, maybe next semester I'll be able to afford the dorms?

THREE HOURS LATER, my teeth are aching from all the forced smiling, my head is spinning, my feet are killing me in these heels, and repeating my internal mantra about *glass half full* is losing its effect.

Worst of all?

Somebody spiked the punch.

At a *wedding*.

How juvenile is that?

I specifically talked to the caterer about having non-alcoholic punch for the, I don't know, *eight* people at this wedding of three hundred who were interested in having a nice beverage not chock-full of vodka or Mom's second best friend, Jack Daniels.

"Embrace the things you cannot control," I whisper, grabbing onto the wall. Because inspirational sayings always help when you're seeing double and your stomach feels like it's about to leap into your throat, right?

"Hey sis," a voice says and then Mr. Winters is suddenly in front of me. I frown. He looks wrong.

I squint. "Your face isn't right. Too smooth." I reach up and touch his head. "And your hair's long."

He laughs. "It's Dominick, not Paul."

"Paul?"

"Whoa." He pulls back from me. "Somebody has been sampling the punch. Hello vodka."

"No!" I grab his arm in alarm. "I don't drink." I shake my head vehemently. "Never. It's evil. Evil stuff. Never. Never ever *ever*."

"Okay. Got it. Whoa, careful there!" He grabs me by the waist when I topple forward. I was shaking my head so hard I lost my balance.

"Oh. Sorry." I put my hands against his chest as I right myself and stand up straight again.

"It's okay." He moves his grip from my waist to my shoulders now that I'm steadier. "I'm here to get you for the Father-Daughter Dance. Do you think you're up for that or do you just want to turn in? I can take you back to the house now if you want."

I stare up at him. The ballroom is dark, lit only by lanterns and twinkly lights overhead. Everything is so nice and swirly. "You're really pretty," I confess, reaching up to touch his smooth cheek. No shadow of a beard there. "And sweet. I'm sorry I thought you were a douchebag."

His bark of laughter is so loud it makes me jump. But it's a nice sound too. "Good to know. Here, let's get you to Dad."

I nod and sink against him as he puts a hand to my back and leads me across the ballroom floor.

His father is standing by the bar chatting with the bartender as we approach. I freeze up just seeing him.

"Wait." My feet scrabble against the floor as I resist Dominick's forward motion. He finally stops too. I look up into his face, so like his father's, but not at the same time.

"He intim— inmimi—" I break off in frustration. My tongue's not working right. "'Milimat—" I open my mouth and stretch my tongue to try to make it work better.

"Intimidates you?" Dominick supplies.

"Yes! That." I point at him and nod. "Exactly."

"Don't worry," Dominick starts moving us toward his father again. "He won't bite." Then he leans in and whispers, "Unless you ask him to."

I whip my head around. "What?"

But we're already to Mr. Winters.

"Sarah, so good to see you finally." Mr. Winters takes my hand as Dominick delivers it over to him. I look back but Dominick almost immediately disappears into the crowd. My mouth dries at his quick exit.

I'm all alone. With Mr. Winters. Paul. His first name pings like a bell through my head.

Though of course we're far from alone. There are three hundred of Mr. Winters's, my mother's, and Grandfather's closest friends and associates all around us.

So why do I feel like Mr. Winters is looking at me like I'm the only woman in the room?

Um, girlish fantasies, an overactive imagination, and unresolved daddy issues much?

I groan internally even as I paste on a smile and pull my hand back.

"Where's Mom?" I look around.

"I'm not sure." Mr. Winters doesn't take his eyes off me to search the crowd for Mom, though. His focus stays zeroed in on me. "Around somewhere I'm sure. She was excited about this event. She seemed quite motivated to make it the largest to-do of the social calendar this season." Then he leans in, his eyebrows furrowed in understanding, "Though she may have gotten overwhelmed by it and be stalled out drunk in one of the side rooms somewhere."

His words startle me. I don't get the feeling he says it maliciously. Merely that he's sharing a fact he knows I understand well.

"So...*why*?" I abandon all attempts at social niceties. I drop the sweet smile and take up last night's query. "Why did you do all this? Why marry her?"

The intimidation I felt last night and even moments before is absent. Liquid courage, that's what they call it, right? I hate the lack of control I have over my faculties right now, hate that I imbibed alcohol when I swore on my life I'd never touch a drop of the stuff because of what it's done to Mom—but hey, embrace every path life takes you on, right?

And I really want an answer to this question.

Mr. Winters just reaches out and takes my hand. A zing runs through me from the tips of my fingers and all throughout my body. It's the first time we've ever touched. My eyes shoot up to his.

They're so green. Bright. Fathomless.

Then he nods beyond me. "It's important to your grandfather that you and I get along."

I look behind me and see Grandpa watching the two of us. He nods to me, then to Mr. Winters.

"Time for the Father-Daughter Dance," Mr. Winters says.

I blink, confused even as my hand tingles at the continued

contact of his hand on mine as he draws me out through the dancing couples to the middle of the dance floor.

Was that an answer to my question?

Did he marry Mom because of Grandpa? Because even though Mom's broke and a disgrace, Grandpa still has power, influence, and prestige? He even has influence among several important lobbies in Washington, from what I understand.

I couldn't care less about politics. I mean, I care as much as the normal concerned citizen. You know, I watch the news and my Facebook feed and am generally as disgusted with the whole process as everyone else. I don't know and I don't want to know the specifics of what Grandpa does.

I look back at Grandpa before we're swallowed up in the couples on the dance floor.

"Don't worry about that," Mr. Winters says. "Just dance with me."

This seems like a good idea, especially since as he puts a hand on my waist, lifts my right hand in the air, and we start swaying back and forth, the world starts spinning topsy-turvy again. I grab hold of his lapel at first to try to calm my seesawing stomach before he shakes his head with a gentle laugh. "Sarah, have you ever danced with a man before?"

I'm about to respond that, 'Of course I have.' But then I realize that no, the only time I ever danced with anyone like this was at my high school prom. And Jason was most definitely a boy and not a man. He was my first and only real boyfriend—and believe me, one was enough to put me off them for the rest of high school. They spiked the punch at prom too but at least then I knew to be on the lookout for it and only drank from a bottled water I'd brought with me. Jason proceeded to get sloshed and I spent the night pushing off his handsy, drunken advances.

Such fun.

"No, I haven't." I shake my head.

"Good." Mr. Winters grins at me and for a second he looks more wolf than Viking god.

I blink. What does that mean? This man is my Mom's new husband. We're dancing a *father-daughter* dance. What is going on? I'm so confused. The world is so spinny.

Mr. Winters takes my other hand and places it on his broad shoulder. I stumble, which causes me to lean in to his chest.

He smells soooooooooo good. The cool, crisp smell of his cologne mixed with him and God, his chest just radiates heat.

My head feels heavy, so I lay it down. The material of his tuxedo is soft against my cheek.

He laughs and I feel the deep rumble of it through his chest. And his heartbeat. It's so strong and steady. I like that.

And he's warm. Did I mention that? He's really warm.

I yawn. The music feels like it's coming through water, a background noise to his heartbeat drumming out. Percussion. *Thump, thump, thump, thump, thump—*

Back and forth swaying.

"I think it's time for Cinderella to get to sleep." I hear the rumbled whisper like I'm in a dream. It's such a nice dream.

Until the sourness in my stomach twists and turns in on itself.

I grab at my middle with both hands. "I don't feel so good."

"Aha," Mr. Winters says, one hand still on my waist. "That definitely means an end to the ball."

I blink and look around me, rousing out of my foggy state. Oh God, I feel miserable and I'm in a room of veritable strangers. None of these people are my friends.

The ugly truth?

I don't have any friends. Lots of acquaintances. No real friends.

I'm alone in the world.

I stumble away from Mr. Winters toward what I hope is the edge of the dance floor.

Uber.

Yeah. That's what I need.

Get an Uber.

Just need phone.

I reach for my pocket.

Except this dress doesn't have any pockets. Crap. Stupid dress.

I hate dresses. I never wear them.

How do I get Uber without my phone?

Why do the lights keep spinning? I sway on my feet, still clutching at my stomach as I take another stumbling step forward through the crowd.

"Whoa, Cinderella." Strong arms come around me from behind.

Warmth. Such lovely warmth at my back. His deep rumbly voice is there again and immediately the anxious stress and confusion I felt just moments ago melts away.

"Where do you think you're going? Why don't you let Dominick and I help you get home?"

"But—" I look back. Dominick stands behind his father. They have mirrored looks of concern on their chiseled, handsome faces. I look back and forth between them, struck dumb for a moment. But then I remember my objections.

"The party." I frown. "It's for you. Just need my phone. An Uber." I blink and look up into Mr. Winter's green eyes. "I'll be f-fine. I always am."

His eyebrows draw together at that. Immediately I want to shrink away. He looks upset by what I said. Have I disappointed him somehow?

Of course you have, Sarah. You've just gotten embarrassingly drunk at the man's wedding and no doubt you're making a huge scene right now.

I glance around to see who's watching us. "I'm sorry," I whisper, looking to the floor, completely horrified. Oh God, I really am my mother's daughter.

"Stop it." A large hand comes underneath my chin and gently urges my face up. Even in my muddled state, the point of connection where Mr. Winters touches me lights me up inside. "No more of that nonsense. Now, we're going to get you home safe and sound."

Dominick nods where he stands beside his father, his face resolute. "I've got her purse and wrap. We're good to go."

Mr. Winters nods and takes my arm. "Just hold onto me and keep your head high as you can. None of these people matter, but you always keep your head high. You're a queen. Remember that, sweet girl."

I swallow hard, but do as he says even as I clutch at his arm like a lifeline. Dominick walks on the other side of me. With the two of them continuing to flank me on either side as we exit the ballroom, shielding me from any accusatory or judging eyes, I do manage to hold my head up. I try to walk as normally as possible and only stumble once. Mr. Winters holds me steady so that by the next step, we're continuing to glide forward so smoothly I'll pretend to myself it was hardly noticeable to anyone watching.

And before I know it, we're outside. The cool air of the night breeze is so welcome on my overheated cheeks. I breathe it in deep, but only manage a couple of breaths before my churning stomach makes me groan and grab at my middle.

"I think I'm gonna—" That's all I manage to get out before bending over and heaving into the bushes that line the hotel walkway.

Both Dominick and his father immediately spring to action. One of them holds me up and the other gathers my hair and pulls it back from my face.

Another deep heave wracks my body and my body expels even more of the poison. I collapse to my knees. Or would have if Mr. Winters didn't have most of my weight and guide me down gently to the concrete sidewalk. It's Dominick holding my hair back, I note miserably before I'm heaving some more.

It's a good five minutes before it finally seems to be done.

Dominick produces a handkerchief. I hate to ruin it, but at the same time I'm eager to clean up. I wipe my mouth and they help me back to my feet. Mr. Winters pulls me to his body. I have no energy to argue that I must be a mess of makeup and tears. I just collapse against his chest. When he runs his fingers through my hair that's long fallen out of its loose updo, it feels like heaven.

One of them must have called the car around, because we only have to walk a few steps to a waiting limousine that pulls up on the curb.

I'm so exhausted I only barely question the fact that Mr. Winters slides into the long seat along with Dominick and I.

Oh no, his wedding...!

But he closes the door and it's obvious he means to go with his son to take me home. Again, the two men flank me on either side.

A Sarah sandwich. The stupid thought makes me giggle.

Mr. Winters flashes his hundred-watt grin at me. "After all that, what's making you laugh, sweet girl?"

I put a hand over my mouth, mortified. "Nothing," I whisper, then fumble for my seatbelt. Do limos have seatbelts? My fingers feel dumb as I reach blindly over the seat. I'm in the middle, so where—

"Here you go, sweets," Dominick says, reaching across my lap and pulling a strap across me. He's taken off his tuxedo jacket and his scent assaults me.

Holy crap.

He smells really good. It's a different cologne than his dad wears. But really... just, yum. I'm shocked that anything can smell good to me with how nauseated I was a few minutes ago. But damn, that boy smells edible. My eyes track him as he pulls back and buckles me in.

Then I lean back against the plush leather seat and close my eyes. God, my thoughts are all over the place. I need to let this horrible alcohol wear off and get out of my system. Then I can be my normal, in-control self again.

Yes, I'll just rest a little bit.

The limo starts up. The darkened glass between the driver and the back seat is up so I can't see him. It's like a quiet little room all our own back here. Quiet and isolated and safe from all the world. Dominick and his father are so warm beside me.

I feel so warm...and safe...and...

"WAKE UP SLEEPING BEAUTY." The low rumbled whisper is soft, it's easy to pretend it's just part of my dream. A handsome Viking knight has come to save me from the wicked, wicked Queen Mother, who has locked me up in a high tower. The knight has the blondest hair and the greenest eyes—wise eyes full of bright intensity. When he looks at me, I feel like he's piercing straight down to my center. He can see all my desires, even the dark ones that I want to hide from all the world.

I turn and nestle into my warm mattress.

"I think she's happy where she is, Dad."

The voice is familiar. I'm in one of those dreams where I'm aware I'm dreaming but I don't want to come out of it yet. I look up and there, beside the first Viking knight is a second knight, equally handsome as the first, but younger. Where the first gives off an aura of wisdom and the feeling that he'd fight the whole world to keep me safe, the second is all fire and lust. He stares at me with open want, longsword flashing in the light.

Together they race forward and free me from the chains the Queen Mother tied me to the bed with. And then, in turn, they grab my face and drop their lips to mine, one after the other—

My eyes fly open, a hand going to my stomach.

"Are you feeling sick again?" I look up into Mr. Winters's concerned eyes. Which is when I realize my head is in his lap.

That's right. Somehow during the limo ride, I've managed to lay out on the seat—my head in Mr. Winters's lap and my thighs thrown over Dominick's legs. Mr. Winters's left hand lays casually on my head, his hand playing with a lock of my auburn hair right below my ear.

I jerk upright, pulling away from both of them.

"You all right?" I register Mr. Winters's question through my mortification.

"I'm fine." I wince. Actually, I feel like hell. "Or, I will be. I just need some sleep." Then I feel my cheeks flame. "In my bed," I clarify, then I feel stupid. Because obviously that's where I *should* be sleeping. Not nestling up against these two men who are still basically strangers to me.

Dominick apparently reads something of what I'm feeling on my face because he rubs my shoulder. "We're family now. This is what family does. We help each other out. It's okay." His other hand joins the first until he's giving me a gentle back rub that does feel divine. I have to fight the urge to relax back against him.

"I should go inside," I say, looking back to Mr. Winters. "And you should be getting back to the party." Suddenly my brain catches up and I realize all the implications of what my little stunt has interrupted. "Oh my God." My hand flies up to cover my mouth. "Your wedding night!" I all but stumble to get to the limo door and shove it open. "Let me just—"

Both Mr. Winters's and Dominick's sudden laughter cuts my panicked movements short.

I look back at them like they're the ones who drank too much.

But Mr. Winters's eyes are still amused when our gazes meet again.

It's Dominick who fills me in on the punch line I was missing. "Sorry sis, didn't anyone tell you? This isn't one of *those* marriages. It's not exactly a love match."

I frown. Well, I obviously knew enough to realize that, but then what—

Mr. Winters reaches out and takes my hand. "Your mother and I realized we could come to a mutually beneficial arrangement by marrying one another. I could give her and you some financial stability and I could get... other benefits."

"Like what?" I scrunch my forehead. And then I remember what dots I connected earlier. "Grandpa's influence."

Mr. Winters eyes me for a second and nods. "Exactly."

I sit back on the limo seat opposite the two of them. "What do you need Grandpa for?"

Mr. Winters relaxes his elbows on his knees and laces his hands together underneath his chin. "Do you know the influence your Grandpa has?"

I nod, then pause and shake my head. "Not all of it."

"Well, the oncology department at my hospital is looking to fund a new wing of the hospital and we're short of our goal. I need your family's name to open those doors for me."

Okay. So the mystery is finally solved. And my head is starting to pound and the inside of my mouth is just...ugh. Time for bed.

Still, the devil in me compels me to ask one last question. "So you and my mom...you never...you know..." I look at the floor of the limo and scrape the toe of one of my strappy shoes against the other.

"No." Mr. Winters's voice is firm. "And we never will. I don't mean to be offensive, but I'm just not sure how..." he looks around the limo like he's searching for a politically correct term, "*hygienic* that would be? So no." He shakes his head, his mouth turning down like he's disgusted even by the thought of touching my mother in that way. "Never."

A ridiculous wave of relief rushes through me at his words.

"Well, as enlightening as this discussion has been," Dominick says, opening the door on his side of the limo, "I think little sister's bedtime was about an hour ago." He smiles at me, but it's more of a challenging smirk.

I narrow my eyes at him but in all honesty, I can't disagree. When he holds out a hand, I take it and allow him to slide me along the bench seat toward the door and help me out. His dad follows right behind me.

This weekend the two of them will be moving all their stuff into the South End townhouse where Mom and I live. The brownstone has been in the family for three generation. It's huge and I'm sure would be worth a crazy amount—luckily Grandpa still holds the deed so Mom couldn't sell it.

The valet brings in two large duffels behind us as we make our way up the stairs. I guess that's what the guys will be living out of until the rest of their things arrive in a couple days.

Thankfully, they help me up the stairs to the door. My heels are killing me and I still don't feel too steady on my feet.

And finally, we're inside. I survived the day. I kick off my heels in the entryway and glare at the ornate stairwell. It would be fine if I just crashed on the downstairs couch for just *one* night, right?

I'm sure I didn't say that last thought out loud, but as if he can read my mind, Mr. Winters suddenly sweeps me off my feet. *Sweeps me off my feet*—I'm not kidding. One of his arms goes underneath my knees and the other under my back. Instinctively, my arms clutch around his neck.

Once again, my body is pressed against the furnace of his body. But my head is clearer than it was earlier in the night so I don't sag against him and lay my head on his chest. No matter how tempted I am.

Plus, God, I'm aware of what a mess I must be. My eyes watered when I was throwing up earlier so my makeup must be a mess, and I can only imagine the rats nest that my hair is, not to mention my breath—

I clamp my mouth shut and resolve to only breathe out through my nose until Mr. Winters puts me down.

I don't have to worry about it for long, though.

Mr. Winters bounds up the stairs as if I'm no heavier than tissue paper. Now, I am petite, but *still*. He's running up the stairs basically bench pressing me. And by the time he gets to my room and finally sets me down on my bed, he still hasn't even broken a sweat.

That's it. Theory affirmed. He's secretly a Viking god parading as a hospital oncology department administrator.

I *knew* it.

Dominick comes in right behind him.

"Thanks," I blush so hard I'm sure I can feel it to the tips of every hair follicle.

I sit on the edge of my bed, my ugly orange dress crinkling in the sudden silence. Both men just look at me. Dominick's smiling at me affably, but his father's watching me with an intensity that makes me—I don't know, feel hot and at the same time creates little chills that run up and down my spine.

He's not sleeping with Mom. The thought comes out of nowhere but pings back and forth like a pinball going crazy and lighting up little neon signs all over my head. He never has and, from the apparent disgust on his face when he talked about the subject, he never will.

I look down at my toes. I got a pedicure for Mom's big day so for once, my feet look pretty. I hide one foot under the other. Fidgety. Suddenly I'm feeling far too sober.

"Okay, well." I break the heavy silence. Maybe I'm the only one finding it awkward? I glance up at the two men studying me as if I'm an intensely fascinating TV channel. "I'm going to get cleaned up and head to bed." I give a short little wave. Oh God, well I just amped the awkward up to a whole new level. "Thanks for everything. Night."

"All right, sweet girl." Mr. Winters smiles at me like he's amused by me, then leans down and presses a kiss to my forehead.

Dominick follows his lead and pulls me close with his hands on my shoulders. Then he kisses me so far back on my cheek it's almost on my ear. It's not a quick little peck either. It's a slow press of his lush, wide lips. "Sleep tight, little sister," he breathes low into my ear. Then he kisses me again, even closer to my earlobe.

By the time he pulls back I'm almost trembling, eyes wide. The feeling I had low in my stomach when I woke up with my head in his father's lap is back. A deep swooping sensation that feels connected to parts even lower and—

What is going on—?

But he and his father both have the same smiles they did moments ago, like everything that's happened tonight is perfectly normal. And then, without another word, Dominick heads out the door, his father following.

TWO

Life with Dominick and Mr. Winters in the house is strange at first, but I quickly get used to the routine of having two extra people around. I was dreading it before the wedding—while the brownstone is big by Boston standards, it's still only four thousand square feet. But I find that I don't have to hide out in my room or stay at the campus library for all hours of the night like I'd been planning before the boys moved in.

It turns out it's actually *nice* having more people in what was always an empty, hospital-like space.

Mom went through a phase where she was obsessed with white as a decorating scheme. Therefore, all the walls are white. The furniture. The art. Vases. You name it, it's white.

"I'm in a hospital where I'm surrounded by white," Dad declared on move-in day. And then he and Dominic proceeded to carry in all kinds of eclectic furniture and place them all throughout the house. Worn leather chairs and overstuffed couches that were actually—*gasp*—comfortable to sit on.

And, oh yeah, sidebar: Mr. Winters asked me to start calling him Dad after about six weeks. He said it was too awkward for me to keep referring to him as Mr. Winters—it was far too formal. And *Paul* didn't sound right either. So why not try out Dad? That was, if I was comfortable with it?

I was probably far too readily accepting of the intimacy. Calling him Mr. Winters, or even Paul...that just meant he was some guy who happened to be living with us. But 'Dad'...it makes it, I don't know...*real*. Like he's actually family. *My* family even if he's not Mom's.

They avoid each other. Mom stays out all hours of the night and then sleeps all day, only to wake up in the late afternoon to make herself ready to go out all night again. She's got money again, though Dominick told me Dad's given her a strict allowance. They have different bedrooms. I heard them say a few words to each other the other night, but that's been the extent of their interaction that I've seen.

No, it's Dad, Dominick and me that are the family.

We all leave the house at different times of day so we don't usually see each other for breakfast. Dad's usually up the earliest of any of us to make it to the hospital. Dominick's just started his residency at a different hospital. He's training to be a cardio-thoracic surgeon. Both he and his dad are so crazy smart. Dominic graduated from high school a year early and then raced through college doing a combined Bachelor/MD program. Sometimes when they get to talking at the dinner table about the things Dominick is learning, it's hard not to feel intimidated.

But then the next second, Dad's asking me about what I'm learning at college. Talking about my early education and learning theory classes seems a bit, well, juvenile compared to saving lives, but both Dad and Dominick have a way of making you feel like you're the most important person in the room.

No matter where our days take us, we always make sure to meet back up for dinner. No matter if that's at six-thirty or ten o'clock. We can't manage it every day. Dominick has twenty-eight hour shifts sometimes. I always heard that doctors-in-training had insane hours, but getting to see it up close and in person makes me appreciate all the more what a sacrifice it is to become the best of the best in his field.

Dad told me it's one of the reasons he moved into administration—the hours were so punishing. One day, he said he woke up and wondered what he was doing it all for. He ended up realizing he'd rather spend more time with his son and enjoy the years he has left on this earth.

Dominick obviously feels differently at this point in his life. Then again, he's only twenty-four.

I look up from the chicken marsala I'm stirring when Dominick calls out in a loud voice, "Honey, I'm home!" from the entryway. It took me awhile to distinguish their voices. Dad's has a slightly lower, scratchier quality.

The kitchen is behind the main living room beside the entryway, so Dominick's voice comes through loud and clear.

"In here," I call back. "Hope you're hungry."

Dominick's heavy footsteps sound as he walks across the hardwood toward the kitchen. Even without his shoes on, I swear he always lumbers everywhere he goes. Dad is totally the opposite. I never hear him and then all the sudden he'll appear in a room behind me, inevitably startling the crap out of me. It's become a game with him. I swear he gets a fiendish delight every time I jump out of my socks.

"I'm starved," Dominick says. His eyes certainly appear hungry as he eyes me. He looks me up and down, from the tips of my bare feet up my legs to the short boy shorts I'm wearing, up my tank top where he pauses on my cleavage, then to my face.

And finally he glances down at what's in the pan.

My mouth has gone completely dry. My cheeks are hot.

Because I'm cooking, of course. It gets hot in the kitchen when I have the stovetop on like this. That's all.

I stir the marsala and pull it off the burner to the side of the stove.

And I pretend I didn't just catch my stepbrother ogling me.

"Where's Dad?"

I swallow, then smile up at Dominick. "Showering. He barely beat you getting home."

Dominick nods and leans back against the counter. That's when I notice just how tired he looks. He just came off a double yesterday and then had to go in again today.

"Hey," I walk over to him. "You doing okay?" I bump my shoulder into his. "You sure this new schedule isn't too much?"

Even with his eyes closed and his head tipped back, I see his jaw tense. "I can do it. I have to. There are only four spots in the advanced cardio-thoracic residency program at Boston General. I am *going* to get one of them."

"I know you will." I'm not just blowing smoke up his backside either. I can't imagine anyone else who works or studies harder than Dominick. He just started his residency but already he's thinking about advancing. He's good enough too, from what Dad says, even though he's the youngest of his fellow residents. My first impression of him as a pretty playboy was completely wrong. He never goes out or parties. Every night he's home, studying or sleeping. He never gives himself a break.

I lift his arm and nestle in for a hug. I squeeze him tight around his middle. "There's no way you won't get it. You work your ass off and you're a genius. Plus, you genuinely *care* about the people you come across every day. I know you could barely sleep the other night, you were worrying so much about Mr. Nunez after his surgery last week."

Holding him as tight as I am, I feel the huge expulsion of air as he breathes out what feels like a mountain of stress.

"Damn. You always make me feel better. How do you do that?"

Does he have any idea how happy his words make me? That I'm able to affect his mood and make things even an iota better for this amazing man, God, that's everything. I turn my face up toward him and grin so hard I'm pretty sure my face will break.

He smiles down at me. It's breathtaking. Heartbreaking, because he still looks so tired. Always so weary. I wish I could *really* make it better for him in more than just a surface way.

"I love seeing my two kiddos getting along so well."

I jerk away from Dominick at hearing Dad's voice. I look up and see him standing in the doorway of the kitchen. I don't even know why. It's not like we were doing anything wrong. It's just— I— I mean—

"The marsala's ready," I blurt, turning away from both of them.

"Smells delicious," Dad says.

"Thanks," I say, my cheeks heating stupidly as I reach up and grab plates from the cabinet. When I turn back to get the rice and marsala to dish out, music plays from Dad's ipod that he's set in the dock by the window—the blues, like he always puts on when it's his turn to choose the music. Dominick's busy setting silverware by the plates.

I can't help pausing and just watching the two of them. A woman's deep, soulful voice rings out from the speakers, providing the perfect soundtrack to the moment. God, I can't believe that at nineteen, I've finally found the family I never had.

Dad sees me watching him and smiles. He comes over to me and lifts my right hand up, his other hand moving to my waist just like he did at the wedding. Then he pivots and before I know it, we're dancing around the kitchen. I let out a little yip of surprise and then laugh as he spins me out and then back into his chest.

The song changes to a faster tune and when Dad spins me again, he lets go. I almost cry out but needn't have worried. Dominick is right there to catch me. He expertly picks up where his father left off. More familiar with the form now, my right hand immediately lifts and Dominick's is there to meet mine.

We dance and spin a few times and then right as the jazzy number reaches a frantic chorus, Dominick dips me to the floor.

Naturally, this elicits another squeal out of me.

Dominick rolls me back up to standing and pulls me so close that when we're chest to chest, I can feel just how hard he's breathing.

And then, as suddenly as he first grabbed me, he releases me. "Let's eat before the delicious food you made gets cold."

I step back, nodding and hoping I don't look as flustered as I feel.

"You sit," Dad says, putting his hands on my shoulders and giving a quick massage as he directs me toward my chair. "I know you've had a long day too, and you cooked. Let us take care of you for once."

"Oh, that's not necess—"

"Sweet girl," he says, his tone warning. "I insist."

He puts a little bit more pressure on my shoulders once we get to my chair and I sit. It does feel *so* good to get off my feet. I was observing a kindergarten class for a school project, and well, there's no way to simply 'observe' when there are screaming five-year-olds grabbing at your skirt and asking you to color and play with them. I became the unofficial class 'helper' all day. And as adorable as those kids were, I'm pretty sure my ears are still ringing. There was this little blonde girl and that kid had a set of lungs on her and she didn't mind letting the whole world know when she wasn't in a good mood, let me tell ya.

Dominick sets the rice on the table and serves everyone some, followed by Dad with the marsala. The steaming food smells delicious and my stomach rumbles in response. I barely had time to scarf down half the peanut butter and honey sandwich I packed for lunch before there was a crisis on the playground and I had to hurry back to it.

The men sit and then we're all diving in.

Dinner's quiet for a while as everyone digs in. I have a feeling Dad and Dominick were just as hungry as I was with the way they're attacking the mini-mountains of marsala Dominick loaded onto each of their plates with.

Dominick eats with the gusto of a man who's been starved for months.

After about ten minutes, when he's filling his plate for seconds, Dad shakes his head. "Filling up that hollow leg of yours?"

Dad always eats with a calm, measured pace and will sometimes close his eyes with a look of concentration, like he's just thinking about the flavor of his food and how pleasurable the whole act is. I've never been more conscious of my cooking than since he moved in. I want it to be perfect for him.

Dominick acts like the whole thing is a land/speed contest, except you know...with food getting shoved in his mouth. It's even worse in the mornings. He jams food in his mouth as he runs out the door, always in a rush. Apparently before they moved in, he would just eat the worst junk too. And him a *doctor*.

Dominick just grunts and starts shoveling in the second serving. I just shake my head.

Once the beast that is my new brother is finally sated, we start talking about our days. Since it's actually early tonight, Dad suggests we leave the dishes for later and move to the den for dessert and to watch a movie he and Dominick had talked about wanting to see on Netflix.

My stomach warms in delight at the thought of getting to spend more time with them. They've been living here for just shy of three months now and it's rare that we all get to hang out together apart from our daily dinners. I've spent time with each of them one-on-one, but coordinating our schedules for more than an hour a day is difficult without real dedicated effort.

"You guys go ahead, I'll get the chocolate mousse cups." I try to tame my ridiculous grin as they nod and head for the other room. Sometimes I feel like such a dorky little sister. I worry that both of them will realize just how lame I am and how many more interesting places they could be than stuck here at home. Don't they have awesome bars or clubs they could be partying at?

But so far, they both seem to be homebodies. I'm something of a night-owl—probably comes with growing up with Mom—so I'd know if they were coming home late...or not at all. But so far, apart from Dominick's crazy shifts, neither of them seems to have any...extracurricular activities. Dad didn't make any secret out of the fact that he and Mom don't plan to, *you know*, at least with each other. But I haven't seen or heard him mention any other women. Dominick either.

Maybe they're just really discreet or Dominick finds outlets in the hours between work and coming home. Maybe Dominick and one of the other residents at the hospital...? Or they're celibate? Or going through one heck of a dry spell?

Oh my *God*, why am I even thinking about any of this?

I squeeze my eyes shut and bang my head lightly on the refrigerator door. I shake my head at myself. My brain is so weird sometimes, my mind going such strange places.

I open the fridge door and grab three of the little individual chocolate mousse cups I filled earlier right after I got home. They look frosty and delicious and chocolatey. I glance down at the three I have balanced precariously in my hands and set them down on the counter. Then I grab a serving tray, transfer the three cups and reach back in the fridge for a fourth. After getting spoons I head into the den.

Dominick's eyes light up when I set down two cups of mousse in front of him.

"Little sister, you know the way to my heart." He grabs a spoon and eagerly starts devouring the first dessert. "Come sit here by me." He pats the center of the large couch where he's splayed out, his mouth thick with chocolate.

I roll my eyes at him but drop to sit where he says.

He's devoured his whole first cup by the time Dad sits down on the other side of me with the remote.

Their bodies are both so warm, I can't explain the chills that pop up all over my arms.

"Cold?" Dad asks, turning to me. He grabs the soft blanket that's always draped across the back of the couch and wraps it around me, squeezing me in a quick hug as he does.

He's so close I can't help inhaling him. He smells the same as he did that first night at the wedding. My eyelids drop half-closed as I breathe in long and deep.

A secret I would die before admitting to anyone, ever? Sometimes when no one's home, I sneak into Dad's bedroom and smell his shirts. And then go in his bathroom and inhale his cologne. It's not nearly the same thing as being near him like this, so warm and alive and just...*him*. It's always missing something—the lived-in quality of his body, of whatever smell that's just all Dad.

Oh God, it's creepy, isn't it? I'm a creepy, creepy girl and seriously, if anyone ever knew—

But it just makes me feel, I don't know... *Safe*. Sometimes everything gets so overwhelming. I've been carrying everything on my own for so long. And suddenly here are these two guys with me in the house. I'm not alone anymore. But when they're not home, I get a little freaked out and I just need to prove to myself that they're actually *real*.

But tonight, they're here, choosing to spend their evening in with me instead of out in the hundreds of other places they could be, schmoozing with a thousand people more interesting than me.

"Does that feel better?" Dad asks right after taking a bite of his own mousse. His chocolatey breath is warm on my cheek and I want to lean into him.

I nod and smile what's probably a dopey smile.

Up close his brilliant green eyes have a thousand hues and facets. Entire galaxies.

Dad grins in return and I feel it all the way down to my stomach where tingly and happy little fireflies dance around before zinging lower all the way to my toes.

"Look, it's starting," he nods with his spoon toward the screen. It takes a moment, but I finally break away from his mesmerizing eyes and settle in to watch the movie.

Naturally, Dominick has already finished all his chocolate mousse. He lies back against the cushions, feet propped up on the coffee table, one long arm slung the couch behind me. In repose, his posture is almost feline it's grace. Like a sated lion in his lair. Perfectly at ease—but with all that muscle, you get the feeling he's always poised to strike, and strong enough to rip anything apart that stands in his way.

He drops his arm over my shoulders and pulls me into him. "So, sis, do you *really* have space for dessert after that deliciously filling dinner you made?" He eyes my chocolate cup.

Alright, so the predator doesn't seem so scary when he's begging for more dessert. I laugh and push him off me.

"Never get between a woman and her chocolate!" I mock glare him down and raise my spoon like it's a weapon.

He raises his hands up. "I do apologize, ma'am."

"Good," I pretend huff and settle back into the couch. I eat my first spoonful and *oh my God*, am I glad I defended my dessert. My eyes immediately close as I savor the rich chocolate cream on my tongue. S*ooooooooooooo* good.

A choked cough from beside me makes my eyes pop open.

Only to find both Dominick and Dad staring at me.

"What?" I ask, flipping the spoon over and licking it to get the last bits of cream off.

Dominick sits up a little straighter and grabs one of the side pillows. He lays it across his lap.

I eye him. "Don't look at me like that. You are so *not* getting this chocolate cup."

"Right," he says, and for some reason his voice sounds a little strangled. "Oh look, the starting credits are done." He points back at the screen. "Don't want to miss the beginning."

I frown at him. He seems a little stiff, but whatever. He's right, the movie is starting. I turn my attention to it and continue eating my chocolate.

The movie begins normally enough. A middle-aged but still handsome college professor goes about his normal morning routine. His wife harangues him about not having enough money to go on vacation with her friends to the Cape while he shaves. By his expression, you can tell it's an old argument.

At the breakfast table, his teenage kids ignore him when he tries to engage them in favor of staring at their phones.

He drives a car that's seen better days to a small picturesque college. He walks into class looking as weathered as his car.

And then he sees her.

A coed sitting in the middle of the very front row.

She's wearing a tight, red sweater. Red lipstick.

His eyes zero in on her. The music changes. Everything slows down.

It's a bit cinematically obvious, but still effective. And the chemistry between the two actors makes it work.

A slow smile creeps over her face when she notices him staring. She bites on the tip of her pen coyly. He clears his throat and turns on his laptop connected to the projector. He begins the lesson on Renaissance literature. She listens with rapt attention.

All throughout class, not-so-subtle glances are exchanged.

It's a slow, tension-filled build up from there. By the time they actually kiss thirty minutes later, my hands are clenched together in my lap and my stomach is tight.

Then, for all the slow build, it explodes. The professor shoves everything off his desk and slams her down. Seconds later he's shoved up her skirt and his pelvis slams back and forth against hers.

My breath hitches in shock.

I mean, I suspected the pair would eventually... but...he's her *teacher*. It's so...

I blink, unable to tear my eyes away from the actor as his face contorts in pleasure and determination.

It's not pretty or romantic like I've often seen sex depicted in movies. He's just sort of jamming himself in and out of her. The coed looks just as shocked as I feel. For all her bravado in seducing him, now that it's actually happening, she seems, I don't know—unprepared. Or maybe just blown away by it all.

God, it's just a movie, Sarah. Stop thinking about it so hard. They're just really good actors.

But... things like this *do* actually happen in real life all the time. You always hear about teachers and students. Scandals in the news. My legs shift and I twist them together, feeling that strange liquidy feeling at my apex that happens when I think about sex.

I all but jump out of my skin when Dominick reaches down and grabs one of my sock-clad feet.

"W-what are you doing?" I hiss. My voice is barely audible above the grunts and pleasured gasps coming out of the surround sound speaker system.

Dominick looks up at me with the most innocent expression—like almost intentionally or mockingly innocent. "What? You told us you were on your feet chasing those little monsters around. I know how much my feet hurt after being on them all day. You cooked. Let me do something nice for you." He starts massaging my feet. The protest dies on my tongue when he rubs my arches in deep little circles with his thumbs since *God*, that does feel *amazing*.

Then I just have to close my eyes. Watching the sex scene while Dominick touches me? That's too many things to compute at once. After a few minutes I hear the characters on screen start to talk normally again and I open my eyes.

Only to find that the man has brought the girl back to his house. None of the rest of his family are home. They stop by the kitchen before heading upstairs. At first I'm confused because they bring what looks like a bag of groceries with them to his bedroom.

I quickly figure out what the groceries are for. Whipped cream, chocolate sauce, strawberries, kiwi, and one very strategically employed banana.

Pretty sure my jaw is permanently dropped open for the next thirty minutes of the movie. At one point I have to tilt my head sideways because I didn't know the human body could contort that way. The actress must be a ballet dancer or some kind of contortionist in her other life.

The mild-mannered professor has completely disappeared and in his place is a dark, commanding presence. The tables have completely turned from the beginning of the movie.

When he takes her to a sex club, I can barely breathe.

And then suddenly the movie pauses.

I turn to look at Dominick who has my calf in his hand. "Why'd you stop it?" My voice is high-pitched, half-panted.

It's dark in the den. Dad turned off all the lights for the movie and with just the light from the TV, I can't make out the expression on Dominick's face.

"Your breathing was getting a little strained," Dad says from the other side of me. He puts his hands on my shoulders, massaging like he did earlier in the kitchen. Except his whole body is at my back now, and with what we've all just spent the last hour watching, my lower body jolts at the contact.

"And you're so jumpy," Dominick says, running one of his hands up and around the bottom of my calf, squeezing as he goes. My eyes jerk open wide as he rubs and kneads my flesh between his two large hands. "I thought maybe the movie was getting to be too much for you."

"Oh," I squeak out. Both of them are touching me. Oh God. Oh my God. It feels amazing. But wrong.

No, it's just the way that I'm feeling about how they're touching me that is wrong. Dominick's a doctor. Of course he knows how to give an amazing massage. My feet and lower legs have never felt so loose—truly a miracle since the rest of my body is winding tighter and tighter.

"You really have some tension up here," Dad murmurs, kneading my shoulder. "You've been studying too hard. It's the weekend now. Time to relax and let go of all that. You're home now. With family." He rubs around to my collarbone and pulls me back into his chest. "Shh, that's right, sweet girl." He shifts me so I'm cradled in his arms. "You must be so tired."

It feels amazing to be cocooned in him.

And also *miserable*.

Because those tingles between my legs? Not just tingles anymore. I'm downright *pulsing* down there. The need to twist, to find some kind of friction—

And screw *everything up* all because of my *stupid*, inappropriate... I can't even finish the thought.

I jerk away from Dad and pull my legs out of Dominick's hold. The blanket falls away from my shoulders as I jump to my feet.

"I'm gonna go to bed now," I blurt without looking at either of them. "See you tomorrow. I'll make pancakes if anyone's around."

And then I make a beeline for the stairs. As in, speed-walk as fast as possible, do not pass go, do not collect two hundred dollars, get my butt upstairs, close my door and stand with my back against it breathing hard and no doubt leaving the two of them wondering about what a complete freak I am.

"One hundred percent freakdom," I whisper to myself, then bang my head against the door before going to wash up and brush my teeth.

Ten minutes later I'm under the covers with the lights off, still feeling like the most miserable excuse for a sister and daughter.

Especially since that feeling down there? The pulsing is still just as intense as it was when they had their hands on me. The more I tell myself not to think about it, the worse it seems to get.

Do *not* think about how strong and sure Dominick's hands felt when he caressed up your calves.

Oh my God, what is *wrong* with me? *It wasn't a caress, dumbass.* He was giving you a massage. He was being clinical. I work out by jogging and my calves get tight. I bet he could feel how knotted up I am.

As soon as my logical self explains this, though, the image flashes: Dominick's hand moving up past my knee, higher, caressing up my inner thigh. Then further still.

I gasp and my back arches.

I suck my lower lip into my mouth and my hand travels down my stomach. Into my panties. I squeeze my eyes shut in shame, but it doesn't stop my fingers from seeking that spot.

All the breath in my lungs expels as soon as I make contact. With my eyes shut, I can so clearly imagine it's Dominick touching me there, that blond mop of hair of his sweeping to the side as he grins at me. So pleased to please me.

Feel good, little sister? I imagine him whispering.

I writhe against my hand.

Oh God, so wrong. All of it. I hate it whenever I give in to touching myself like this. It's dirty and base and I detest everything about it. I walked in on my mom doing it to herself while on her laptop camera for some guy when I was barely a teenager. I was so disgusted, I swore I'd never—

But that movie tonight. And the way the boys were holding me, I just can't stop. My hips jerk forward and back as I buck against my hand.

My door creaks open.

I freeze and look toward the door. Oh God, oh God, *oh God*, did one of them hear me? I could have sworn I wasn't making any noises but what do I know? No one's ever been in the house before when I've—

I jerk my hand away from myself but then am mortified as either Dominick or Dad's shadow appears in the doorway. What if they saw the movement and guessed at what I was doing? Or the smell. Can they smell...you know? My aroma?

I shove my face into the pillow but then realize that's stupid. Obviously whichever one of them it is knows I'm awake. I've been moving and spazzing all over the place.

"What's up?" I ask, though my voice comes out more like a high-pitched squeak.

"You ran off so quick." Dominick's voice. He steps in the room and closes the door behind him. "I wanted to make sure everything's okay."

He steps closer, his face cast in heavy shadow with just the light of my nightlight in the room.

I'm nineteen. Far too old to be afraid of the dark. Still I haven't gotten rid of my childhood fairy nightlight.

And while I'd been, *you know*, I had my eyes squeezed shut tight, so my eyes never got a chance to adjust to the dark. I can only barely make out Dominick's features.

He comes closer and sits on the edge of the bed. "So are you okay?"

It's then that I realize I never answered his question.

I nod my head furiously, then realize his body is blocking the light and he might not be able to see me either. "Mmm hmm," I vocalize. I don't exactly trust my voice at this point. I clutch my blankets up tighter around my face, but then, oh *God*, I can smell myself on the hand I was touching myself with. I jerk it back down deep underneath the covers.

Thank God it's so dark in here. Dominick can't see the cherry red my cheeks are no doubt turning.

"You sure?" Dominick sounds skeptical.

"Totally sure," I say.

He sighs and leans back against my headboard.

Why is he still here? He just needs to *leave*. Leave me to my misery and stupidity and—

"Well to tell the truth, I haven't been doing so great."

What? All my obsessive, self-involved thoughts slam to a halt. I sit up and move so that I'm beside him. "What do you mean? What's going on?"

My eyes are finally adjusting to the light and I can see how pensive he is. He's changed into a tank top and sleep pants. He bends his legs and leans his elbows on his knees as he stares sightlessly out into my dark room.

Suddenly I'm glad I used the graduation money Grandpa gave me to redecorate, taking down the pink wallpaper I'd had since childhood and more recent high school boyband posters. Now the room is done in cool green and gold tones.

And then I'm immediately ashamed again that I'm worried about what Dominick will think of my room when he's so obviously distressed.

"You can talk to me, Dom," I put a hand on his forearm. His muscles tense reflexively at my touch but then relax. He reaches over and covers my hand with his.

"I wasn't kidding about what I said earlier," he says, leaning his shoulder into mine. "Everything has been so much better since we moved in here. I feel more..." He pauses like he's searching for a word. "Grounded." He nods.

"So what's bothering you?" I press. I can tell something's eating at him. Talking to him about stuff has always made me feel better over the past couple months. And I want to be that for him—his sounding board, the person he can come to when he needs to unload.

He looks away from me. "I don't know if I can talk about it to you."

My mouth drops open. "You *can*. I promise. No matter what it is. I won't judge." I want him to trust that I can handle it, no matter what *it* is.

He turns back to me. His hazel eyes are so dark when they're in the shadows like they are now. They're the one thing he didn't get from his dad. Right now, his irises and pupils just dissolve into one another in the dim light. "I'm really tired," he says. "But I don't want to leave. Could we... Do you think we could maybe..." he trails off and looks down again.

"What?" I ask. I've never seen him like this. So tentative. He's usually all brash confidence.

"Could I maybe lay down here? I just don't want to leave yet." Even in the dim light, I can see how hopeful he looks. And how afraid of rejection.

I can't believe it. This amazingly strong man, so smart and kind, thinks he could find a little comfort in laying down with me?

"Of course!" I say, scooting over and holding the covers open wide.

If he notices that I'm just wearing a thin-to-the-point-of-sheer spaghetti-strap shirt and white cotton panties, he doesn't comment.

He moves to lie down beside me and pulls the sheet and comforter over him. I always sleep with two pillows. Usually I put one between my legs, but I give that one to him. No, *scratch that*. At the last second, I snatch that pillow back and give him mine instead. What if it smelled like...you know.

"Here," I say, patting the pillow awkwardly as I set it at the top of the bed and then grabbing my leg pillow and settling it under my own head.

Dominick pulls the pillow I gave him under his head and exhales as he settles in. It's as if I can feel the tension leaving his big body beside me.

Meanwhile, I suddenly become aware of every inch of my own skin.

I've never had someone in my bed with me.

Or been in someone's bed.

Yeah, considering the whole prom disaster, my whole *one* boyfriend experiment was short-lived.

But I've imagined this moment a million times. Well, not *this* moment obviously, with my own stepbrother. But a moment like this one. Being in bed with a man, his warmth beside me. Not even doing anything, just *being*. Snuggling maybe.

But none of my fantasies do justice to the real thing.

I'm always so cold. Maybe I have bad circulation or something, but I'm always *freezing*. And Dominick is like a heat machine. I've noticed this about both him and Dad. They run hot. It can be forty degrees out and they'll wear a t-shirt and shorts. Meanwhile I've got long underwear and my giant winter coat on.

"How did your feet get cold again in the ten minutes since I last had hold of them?" Dominick laughs after his shins come into contact with my feet.

"Oh God. Sorry." I yank them away from him. Mortification number three hundred and forty-seven for the evening? *Check.*

"Don't be ridiculous. It's just one of your quirks." Dominick wraps his arm around my waist and pulls me into him.

My eyes sink closed at how good it feels.

So. Much. Better. Than. I. Dreamed.

He fits his knees behind mine and then settles his whole body flush against me.

I'm dreaming.

This is a dream.

I was so tired, and keyed up from the movie. This is obviously an extremely vivid dream.

Because there is no way that Dominick is spooning me in real life.

Is there?

He nestles his chin against the back of my head, moving my hair aside with one hand. "I won't let you be cold, beautiful."

The words are a warm breath against my neck and his arm rests around my waist, curled right below my breasts.

I can't help the next few stuttered gasps that escape my lungs, but then I do everything in my power to concentrate on breathing normally.

Slow breath in, hold for a couple seconds, then slow breath out. There. That's how normal people breathe. Right?

Right??

But Dominick apparently doesn't notice anything off because within two minutes, his breathing regulates and he starts to snore gently. It's simultaneously the most manly and comforting sound I've ever heard. I can feel it rumbling up through his chest at his back. I've never felt anything like it.

Slowly, ever so slowly, I rest my arm over Dominick's where it curves around my stomach. He stirs only the slightest bit and clutches me tighter against him.

My breath hitches again but I don't move my hand from where it lays over his. He settles and his quiet snores start up again.

I lay there for one of the best and simultaneously worst nights of sleep of my entire life. *Best* because I've never felt more secure or beautiful and just... freaking *amazing* in my whole life. And *worst* because I hate that I keep falling asleep. I don't want to miss a moment of it.

I leave my hand over Dominick's as he holds me all night long and know that if it's in my power, I'm never going to let him or Dad go.

THREE

Dominick's sleepovers become a semi-regular thing over the next few weeks. Granted he's still working crazy hours for his residency, so it's maybe two to three nights a week, but God, how I treasure those nights.

If Dad notices our growing closeness, he doesn't say anything, though I do notice his gaze moving between the two of us sometimes at dinner. He doesn't looked concerned, though, just interested as always in what we're doing. I chalk it up to my imagination and paranoia.

It's not like Dominick and I are doing anything *wrong* anyway.

I mean sure, we're sleeping together. But not like *that*!

Dominick will just come in after Dad's gone to bed, maybe after we've all watched TV or he and I study at the kitchen table while Dad works on his laptop. Then Dom and I will talk for a little bit with him sitting against the headboard. I tell him about stuff going on in my life, he tells me about things stressing him out at the hospital, and then he gets into bed beside me and curls me up against him.

I've even actually started being able to fall asleep now since, the more it happens, the more confident I feel that each time won't be the last.

Dominick's not home tonight. Dad's on a business trip. Mom's out as well—*shocker*. It feels like she's gone for days at a time. There will be entire weeks I can go without seeing her. I wonder if Dad doesn't encourage this. The last time I saw the two of them in the same room together he just simply gave her this *look*. Like a 'don't test me' look. I'm not sure what was being communicated, but Mom just lifted her chin and went off in a huff. We didn't see her for four days that time.

Whatever. I finally feel like she's not my problem. And oh my God, it's such a relief. I feel *free*. For the first time in my life. Free and young and just... happy.

Happiness.

What a crazy concept, right?

Well, a little less happy tonight since Dad and Dominick aren't home, but I can't be greedy. I get them so much of the rest of the time.

I yawn as the little scribbled numbers blur on the page. I've been working on this Statistics homework until I feel cross-eyed.

If I'm honest—yes, I wanted to distract myself so I wouldn't miss the boys. The house always used to be this empty, but now it just feels wrong not to hear the TV on or the shower running somewhere or Dom's big clonking footsteps jogging up and down the stairwell. I glance at the clock.

It's eleven. My yawn stretches wider. Okay. I should be able to sleep now.

I wash up, switch on my night light, and turn in.

Dominick sleeps over so much that my second pillow has started to smell like him. I bury my nose in his pillow and inhale. His scent is comforting.

It takes some time, but the math homework did its job and soon I'm nodding off.

...

...

And then I start to dream.

It's one of *those* dreams.

Dominick's big body is curled up behind me. His arm drapes over my waist. Chin nestled in the crook of my neck. Just like always.

It's completely innocent.

Until it's not.

Dominick's hand moves up. His large hand easily envelops my breast. My breasts aren't tiny but they feel that way in his huge hands. And then he gently squeezes—

What the—

Not gentle, not gentle!

He's jerking at my nipple. Pulling and plucking and—

My eyes shoot open.

I'm not alone in my bed.

I swing around to look behind me, confused and just what the—

Dominick.

I blink and breathe and—

"Dominick?"

He's not supposed to be here tonight. He had a double.

But it's definitely Dominick, long floppy hair and all, laying behind me. With his hand on— His hand is on my—

"I need you tonight, beautiful," he whispers and there's something off about his voice. It comes out ragged and choked. "I've tried to fight it, I know it's wrong, but today was just..." He shakes his head, his features contorting. "I need you."

And then he rolls me so that I'm flat on my back and his lips are on my lips. Next thing I know, his body is over mine and his weight is pressing me into the mattress.

His mouth invades mine, pressing for entry.

I, but I—

His hand moves from my breast and drops lower. Before I even have my bearings, one of his thick fingers is pressing at my entrance. Down *there*.

His finger meets wetness and slides right inside me. I gasp in shock as my whole body shudders and pleasure.

That's when I really wake up.

Holy crap.

Dominick is here.

Dominick is touching me.

Dominick is touching me *like that*.

I start kissing him back just as hungrily.

I don't know what's going on. If this is a dream, it's like nothing I've ever— I mean, I never knew anything could even be like—

"God, Dominick," I whisper in between panting gasps. I can't breathe. I'm going to die because I can't breathe. He's stealing my breath. It's so good. So good.

"Fuck, Sarah, say it again," he whispers. His voice still has that deep, desperate quality to it. "You don't know how long I've needed to hear you say my name like that. You've been fucking torturing me."

"Dominick," I breathe out and he lunges against me.

That part of him. I feel it. Hard as a rod. Hot and hard, pressing against my stomach. He swivels and swirls his hips as he kisses me deep.

He pulls back suddenly.

No, God, did I do something wrong—?

But it's only so he can lift me up long enough to pull off my tiny shirt. He pauses for a moment just staring at me. "Holy fuck, little sister. Are you telling me this is what I've been sleeping just inches away from for weeks?" He sounds mesmerized. And his words. I've never known him to be so vulgar.

It's the sexiest thing I've ever heard in my life.

He drops down and starts to suckle one of my breasts, shoving them together with both his hands, licking down the crevice he creates, then taking the other in his mouth.

When he bites down a little on the nipple, I can't help crying out and jerking against him. "That's right, beautiful," he says, licking and then blowing on the nipple he just abused, "let me hear all your noises. There's no one else home. I want it all. I fucking need it."

When he nips at the second nipple, oh God, I do what he wants. I let him hear.

The way he's positioned, lower now, when he pistons his hips forward, his steel rod presses right up against the spot his fingers invaded just a moment ago.

My mouth drops open and my head presses back into the pillow. He alternately worships and tortures my breasts. Meanwhile, he reaches down to caress my hips and thigh and draws my leg around his waist, first one and then the other.

"I want you to ride me, beautiful. Ride me to get off. And don't forget to let me hear it."

His words and his touch and just God, the fact that this is happening at all, this is *really* happening—Dominick is here and he's touching and caressing and *oh*, doing *that*—it all ignites a fire that rages higher and higher.

My legs wrap around his hips and the hardness of him hits the most perfect spot in the universe.

My hips seem to jerk forward and back against him of their own accord. I might have no idea what I'm doing, but my instincts take over.

A drive so intense, oh God, he's sucking on my nipple so hard and pinching the other one. It hurts but feels so, just, what— oh my God, all at the same time, how is that even possible?

But then he releases his hold on both nipples and blows air across them. He drops his hand between us. His finger slips inside me again. Then his thumb rubs and I flex and press against him and he said to let it out so I scream,

"*Dominiiiiiiiiiiiick!*"

Light and heat burst all through my body like ricocheting fireworks. But within my body. I've never felt— I can't— And it just, it keeps going and—

Dominick continues to rub. He buries his head in between my breasts, licking and suckling and tenderly kissing my lips again.

I pant as the light recedes and my consciousness comes back into my body. My fingertips still tingle and when Dominick swirls his thumb around again, my legs spasm with an aftershock. He smiles, but there's still a serious look to his features that's not usually there.

"You did so good, beautiful," he whispers, then kisses my breast again. He moves slightly up so that we're eye to eye, but he doesn't move his hand, occasionally still circling and causing my breath to short circuit.

"Now I need you to be completely honest. I don't care if my question embarrasses you, you have to tell me the truth, no matter what. Can you do that?" His sudden inquiry scares me and with his gaze so direct, I feel like he's looking straight into my soul. Especially after what we just— I mean, God. I've never been more bared to someone. In every sense of the word.

But I nod because it's Dominick.

"How much experience have you had? With sex?"

Heat rises to my cheeks even at the word. Which is silly considering what we— I mean, he just made me—

I swallow. "Not much." I look down.

"Hey." He takes my chin and forces my face back up even as he continues to swirl with his other fingers. Oh my God, *not fair*. How am I expected to even concentrate on anything while he's—

"I need details." His eyes search mine. "I need to know everything you've done. Just how far you've gone with past boyfriends." His jaw tightens on the last two words but then his face softens again as he pushes some hair that's fallen in my face behind my ear.

I feel my cheeks redden further. I don't want to tell him. I couldn't be more inexperienced or immature. I wish he would let me off with the vague answer I already gave, but for some reason, I can see by the look on his face that he feels like he needs to know more.

And after tonight, I have the feeling I'll give Dominick whatever he needs. I shake my head slowly. "I don't have any experience," I whisper.

"So you're a virgin," he clarifies. "Okay, so what about touching and..." He breaks off when I continue shaking my head.

"I mean, I've kissed guys before," I hurry to clarify.

His hands freeze everywhere he's touching me. "But nothing else?" he whispers in clear disbelief. "Not even..." he trails off again and just stares at me.

I can only take so much of being stared at like I'm a side-show act at a carnival. I yank away from him and start to pull the covers up around myself when he rips them away from me.

"God, you're fucking perfect." He grabs me and rolls us so that he's on top. He kisses me deep, that manly part of him pressing even more urgently into me.

He kisses so long and so deep I don't think he's ever going to come up for air. I'm not sure I want him to.

Did I think I was happy before? I didn't *know* happiness.

He finally pulls back, looking slightly anxious.

"What?"

"Well, I want to try something, but I don't know if you're ready."

I hate that he even has to question it.

"I am," I blurt in return. "I'm ready for anything. *Everything.*"

He still looks hesitant. "Do you think you could... maybe just start by..."

"Anything," I repeat, never meaning it more in my life.

He nods. "You could try touching me."

He doesn't have to say any more. I get what he means. Or well, the general idea of what he means. He's not the first to ask, but he's the first I've ever wanted to oblige.

Other boys, like the infamous prom date, have made requests of me throughout the years, with various levels of earnestness and crudeness, to suck their...you know whats.

I've always been disgusted by the whole idea.

Until Dominick.

After what he just gave me, I'm eager to explore his body. Still, my hands are tentative at first as they trail down his muscled chest. I don't want to do it wrong and screw everything up.

Dominick's breath hitches and then he doesn't exhale, like he's holding it waiting for me to go lower. To make contact with it.

Screw it. I'm curious and I don't mean to torture him. I lower my hands the rest of the way until my small fingers close around…

Wow. It's so *big*.

I mean, I've seen a couple of pictures across the years. It's impossible to be a teenager with the internet and not, but he feels so much bigger and wider than any of them looked. And so warm. Not to mention *hard*.

I mean, obviously it was going to be hard. That's the whole point. But I've babysat little boys before and how can *that* grow up to become *this*?

"Christ, beautiful," he hisses out. "Do you know how good that feels? Wrap your little fingers around it and get under the covers with me."

I do as he says, wrapping both hands around him, then feeling up and down the velvety soft skin that covers his hard rod. Oh my God, I'm using romance novel terms, but they are so right. It *does* feel like velvet over a steel rod. I try not to giggle as I lay down beside him.

My attack of the giggles are soon lost in his hands on my body and feeling how he tenses and groans as I rub him up and down, up and down.

"Christ, I love your little hands on me. And watching you just come now." He presses his length in and out of my inexpert fingers gripping him. "You don't know how long we've been looking forward to this."

We?

The question registers in my mind but then Dominick delivers another of his deep kisses. One of his large hands drops to cover mine and he shows me just how he likes to be pleasured. I learn how to twist his shaft and roll my hand up over the bulbous crown. I'm rewarded when I feel a little bit of wetness coat my fingers.

"That's because of how crazy you're driving me, beautiful. Now you try on your own."

I repeat the motions he's just taught me, my brow furrowed in determination as I try to get it right.

"Christ, it's so good," he encourages. "You can squeeze it even harder if you want."

Really? I feel like I'm already choking the life out of the thing but I put all my strength into my grip.

And then I think about how much suction and strength I've heard the human mouth and jaw have.

I want Dominick to be happy with how I'm doing. More than anything else in the universe. And just the thought of licking him. Tasting him. My sex clenches and before I can overthink it or psych myself out, I slip down underneath the covers.

I take him into my mouth and start to suck.

"Holy Christ!" he shouts so loud I'm doubly glad no one else is in the house because if they were, they'd surely come running at his exclamation.

For a second I think maybe I've done the wrong thing after all.

Maybe that's not how you're supposed to do it? Did I bite him accidently or something? I tried to cover my teeth with my lips but maybe I still grazed him and—

But when I try to lift away, Dominick's hand is there putting gentle pressure on my head to keep me in place.

An internal glow flows throughout my body and I lick and suck and lap at his rod. He whispers encouragement and instructions.

Within minutes he's tapping my shoulder.

"Pull off, beautiful."

I do and he presses me back on the bed. Then he tugs himself far more roughly than I ever did, three quick jerks until several hot spurts shoot out and coat my breasts.

"Fuck. Oh fuck," he whispers as the last little bit bursts out of him. He collapses beside me, his hand landing in his cream on my chest. He rubs it all around my chest and down to my stomach.

"You're mine," he says, hazel eyes gleaming as our gazes lock.

My breath hitches as we just stare at each other, both of us catching our breath.

After a few long moments, he reaches for his boxers on the ground and cleans up the mess he made on me.

Then he grabs me close, pulls the sheet and comforter over us, and like always, is out within minutes.

And all I can feel is—*WHAT?*

How does he *do* that? How can he just fall asleep like nothing at all is unusual when we just— just—

I'm still pulsing between my legs. Even though his warmth is behind me now, the memory of him on top of me is still so fresh.

Again—*WHAT?*

He was upset about something when he came in, that was clear.

His words from earlier ring in my head. *I need you tonight, beautiful. I've tried to fight it, I know it's wrong, but today was just...I need you.*

What happened today to set him off like that? And...he's tried to fight it? So I'm not the only one who's had these...feelings.

And sure he said they were wrong too, but what if maybe they aren't. I mean, we aren't *really* sister and brother.

Though even having the thought feels like a betrayal.

No—he is family. He *is*. He's my brother.

But also my...lover?

Oh God this is so messed up.

I squeeze my eyes shut hard, sink back against Dominick, and try to sleep.

And somehow, sleep actually comes. I sleep hard. So hard in fact, that I don't even wake up when sun starts streaming through my bedroom window.

No, I don't wake up until there's an angry voice shouting.

"What the hell is going on in here?"

FOUR

My eyes shoot open only to find Dad standing at the foot of the bed, looking back and forth between me and Dominick with clear shock on his face. Dad's dressed in his usual Saturday attire, khakis and a polo shirt.

Oh my *God*. How late is it? I want to sink into the mattress and die. I jerk the blanket up around myself but still feel entirely exposed.

"Wait, Dad, I can explain," Dominick starts, but Dad is around to his side of the bed in two strides. With no finesse, he jerks Dominick out of the bed and onto the hardwood floor. Dominick is a big man but his father is one of the few men I can imagine almost equaling him in size. Dominick doesn't fight him either. He tumbles down and lands hard on his knees where he stays, completely naked, head bowed.

"I was the one who started coming to Sarah's room," Dominick says heatedly. "She did nothing wrong."

"Is that why she's clutching her blanket around herself in shame?" Dad eyes shoot between me where I huddle on the bed and Dom on the floor.

Tears start leaking out of my eyes at his harsh words. No, this isn't supposed to happen. Everything was perfect. Then it got all screwed up. Dominick's been upset for weeks and I haven't pushed him to *really* talk about it. And if I'm honest with myself, there's a reason I kept wearing such nothing scraps of clothing even when I knew there was a chance he'd sleep over. I'm not *that* naïve. And surely Dominick could feel how I wanted him. Men just know those things, right? Instead of addressing it, I let the tension between us build and build until it just exploded last night. And I hate the way Dad's looking at Dom.

"No, Dad," I sit up straighter, still clutching the blanket tight. "It's all my fault."

Dad's beautiful green eyes flash, then darken as they settle on me. "Is that so? How do you figure?"

"I— I— Well, I—" I glance down helplessly at Dominick, but his eyes are still on the floor. I swallow hard and look back at Dad. No matter how much I want to run away and lock myself up in the bathroom—oh God, is this really happening? Please, *please* let me wake up and this just be a horrible nightmare—

But no, all my frenzied thoughts finally still. *I wouldn't really want that.* Not if it meant giving up last night. I wouldn't erase last night for anything.

I take a deep breath. "It's my fault because I've been getting things confused sometimes. Having the two of you here has been," I pause and hiccup because stupid tears choking up my throat make it too difficult to speak for a moment, "so amazing. I feel all kinds of intense feelings. I can't always sort out what they mean. What Dominick and I—" I look down at Dominick and he finally looks up at me. "I can't lose that."

Dad's voice finally softens. "You won't, baby. But I won't abide a household full of secrets. For that there will be punishment."

I look up at Dad in confusion, but when Dominick gets up off the floor to stand beside the bed, he looks resigned.

"Where?" is all Dominick asks.

Dad points at my desk, then starts loosening his belt. I feel my eyes widen. Surely he's not going to— I mean, Dominick is twenty-four years old!

But sure enough, Dominick bends over and, still buck naked, braces his hands on the edge of my desk.

Dad bends his belt in two, rears back and then there's a loud *crack* as the leather lands on Dominick's ass.

A little screech escapes my mouth but Dominick barely flinches.

"One," he intones.

Another *crack*.

"Two."

"How many?" I ask, feeling unable to do anything except watch on in distress from my bed.

Thwack.

Three.

"Twenty," Dad answers me.

Four through seven land and Dominick jerks a little more with each resounding wallop. Dad seems to swing harder each time too.

Another lands.

"Eight," Dominick says, his voice finally sounding pained. His ass is already bright red. And are those welts I see rising?

"Stop!" I jump off the bed, blanket wrapped around me, and step between Dad and Dominick. "No more."

Dad stops before landing the next blow, looking surprised. Dominick turns around too, expression mirroring his father's.

"Sarah," Dominick says, before reaching out a hand to stop me. I clutch it desperately. He just shakes his head, looking a little confused. "It's no big deal. I did something wrong. I'll take my punishment and learn from my mistake."

I try not to show how stung I feel at his words. I get that what he's going through isn't pleasant. But why is he so quick to call us a mistake?

God, Sarah, put away your own pride. There's a much bigger problem here. Dominick doesn't see anything wrong with his father giving him a beating!

"Dominick, please, just stop—"

But Dominick just nods before bracing his hands on the table again, back in position. "A little rod of correction goes a long way toward improving the child." He sounds like a robot as he says it.

What the—?

I step back from the both of them.

These are two men I care a great deal for. But they have secrets I'm only beginning to glimpse.

Obviously.

"Nine." Smack. "Ten." Dominick's teeth grit and his face is getting as red as his backside. No matter how really, truly, deeply screwed up this all is, I can't stand it for another second.

"Stop it!" I move in between them. "You said it yourself, Dad," I turn to him. "I'm part to blame. Give me the other ten."

Dominick swings around in shock and then his eyes flick to Dad. "No. Dad. Don't."

I follow his gaze and gulp when I see that Dad is obviously considering the idea.

"Sarah, no, you don't need to—" Dominick continues to protest but Dad holds a hand out.

"Sarah's a big girl and both of you were caught in a lie."

I swallow and nod even as my legs go stiff with terror. My eyes drop to the belt. I've never been spanked in my whole life. Mom slapped me a few times when she was especially out of it and high, so it's not that I've been without bruises in my life but... this is *Dad*.

Tears flood my cheeks. It feels like betrayal.

I trusted him. Yeah Dominick and I snuck around and lied, but now Dad's going to *hurt me* for it?

"Hey, look at me." Dad's voice drops to a gentle bass. It's like he can read my mind. "Do you trust me? Would I ever bring you harm?"

He reaches out and takes my hand in his big, warm one.

Instantly the tension leaches out of my body.

He's right. I might be seeing another side to my family, but that comes with getting to know them in a deeper way.

They're letting me in. And he's right, I *do* trust him.

I nod and finally squeeze Dad's fingers back. I look over at Dominick. He looks uncertain but Dad pushes him out of the way.

To make way for me.

Holy crap.

Am I really doing this?

"Assume the position, sweet girl," Dad says, rubbing my neck. "You're going to need to drop the blanket too."

My breath hitches, but even as crazy as all this is, I don't want to let either Dad or Dominick down.

Dominick took his punishment without complaint. I don't want to do any less, no matter how scared I might be.

My whole body shaking, I take a step toward the desk, back toward Dad and Dominick.

I let the blanket fall to the floor. I've never felt more naked in my whole life. One hand drops to cover my shaved sex and my other arm folds up to cover my chest, head down.

Dominick steps close again. "You're doing great," he whispers, reaching down and clasping my hand. "Don't be scared. I'm here."

"Put your hands on the edge of the table," Dad cuts Dominick off. "And don't hang your head, sweet girl. Your body is nothing to be ashamed of."

His words shock me in a way I can't even explain. How can he say that? It was this body that seduced his son. That created this mess in the first place. If I hadn't had all of these…unnatural urges…

"Hands on the desk," Dad's voice reminds me. There's an odd quality to it now. He doesn't sound angry anymore. More like…urgent?

Still shaking and making sure I'm angled just so, in a way that I hope means Dad can see just my back and not my small breasts in profile, I let go of Dominick's hand and tentatively lean forward. I position myself with my hands on the edge of the desk just like Dominick did minutes before.

Smack.

The blow comes almost immediately after I'm in position.

But it's not the sharp bite of a belt. Rather the warm sting of a palm.

Dad just spanked me. With his hand.

"Count or you get twice as many," Dad warns.

Bewildered, I sputter, "One."

His hand comes down again, this time on the other cheek.

"Two!" I squeak.

And so it continues. I can hardly begin to describe the sensation. It doesn't hurt nearly as much as I was afraid of. In fact, it barely hurts at all—it's more of a jolting surprise and sting each time he makes contact. He's not putting his considerable strength into it, I can tell. Nothing like what he was doing when he was belting Dominick. *Thank God.*

Halfway through, my butt just starts to feel really warm and tingly. After seven, Dad pauses and rubs each cheek in turn, kneading and massaging.

Oh my God. What is he—?

It feels—

I blink and then squeeze my eyes shut hard against all the things I'm feeling that I can't sort out.

Abruptly he stops and the spanking continues.

"Eight," I breathe out.

Nine and ten are the most strenuous smacks of all, but then Dad's warm hands are back on my flesh.

My breathing is rapid from exertion, but the exertion of what, I don't know. Holding my muscles still when all I want to do is run away? The mental acrobatics I've been going through over the last five minutes?

"Feel how hot she is, Dominick."

Suddenly, a cooler pair of hands join Dad's warm ones. Both of them are touching my body...

It's official. I never woke up. This is all a crazy dream. For sure.

Then it's just the cooler pair of hands as Dad pulls away. The hair from the back of my neck is lifted up. "Do you want your big brother to make you feel better now?" Dad whispers against my neck, right behind my ear.

My eyes jolt open and I swing my head to look around at him.

The same second I do, Dominick's hands move from my butt to drop underneath and around to my sex. Where he begins to rub at my most sensitive spot.

"She's wet," Dominick says, his voice a low grumble of what sounds like approval.

I try to jerk away from him even as he starts to circle me and one of his big, blunt fingers seeks entrance inside me.

"What are you doing?" I look down at Dom, appalled. Dad is right here. This is what we got in trouble for in the first place—

"It's okay, sweet girl," Dad says, circling my waist with his arms. "I meant it when I said not to be ashamed of your beautiful body. There's no reason for the two of you to hide from me. We're a family."

I'm so absolutely startled by this declaration and by Dad's closeness that when Dominick comes closer and again inserts his finger inside me from below, I don't move away again. I just shudder in pleasure and the sure feeling that I'm doing something terribly elicit and wrong.

But Dad smiles at me, his green eyes bright and brilliant. "That's right, sweet girl. Show Daddy how much you like it. Do you have any idea how much I want you to be happy? It's all Dominick and I want. You've enriched our lives so much, we want to give back to you."

The trembles going through my body get even more violent— both at Dad's words and at the things Dominick is doing to my body. Does Dad have any idea what his words mean to me? I've never— For my whole life I wished someone, anyone would—

"Oh my God!" I whisper and look down. Dominick's replaced his rubbing fingers with his— Oh— God—

His mouth. And it—

Aaaaaaaaaaaah God, I can't even—

My legs buckle at the pleasure but Dad catches me and holds me in his arms. Dominick continues his merciless attack, his tongue circling and lapping and plunging. The pleasure rises higher and higher. I can't— And Dad is right here and—

My mouth opens as pleasure starts to spike through my center.

And that's when Dad leans down and takes my mouth with such hunger, my climax sparks.

Dad kisses me and I kiss him back and Dominick devours my sex.

It's so *wrong* and so *right*.

I hit the highest high, clutching both of them to me as tight as I possibly can.

FIVE

As soon as I come back to earth, I find I'm still in Dad's arms, kissing and being kissed by the most handsome, masculine man I've ever met on earth. And Dominick, my first lover of any sort, still has his head between my legs, licking up my cream as aftershocks jolt in little bursts all through me.

Except these aren't just any two men.

It's my Dad and brother.

Stepdad and stepbrother, okay, but they're so much closer to me than the terms imply.

Oh my God, what we've done is so—

Wrong.

Delicious.

Bad.

Amazing.

Dominick sucks me so hard into his mouth I cry out again right as Dad releases me. I shudder in his arms and he smiles down at me. With one arm still supporting me by my waist, he lifts his left hand to cup my face. His smile is warm and so full of affection. "That's right, baby, give it to us. Give it all to us."

I blink at him, my first impulse to look away. To pull away. I expected...I don't know. For Dad to be ashamed of his impulse.

He just *kissed* me. While Dominick was doing—*that*.

But Dad doesn't look ashamed at all. Only confidently in control. Like there's nothing at all in the world to be worried about. Like everything that's just happened is as natural as breathing. And here, being wrapped in his arms, with Dominick so close as well, it's easy to believe it too.

Dominick caresses his hands up the back of my legs and past my slightly sore buttocks as he gets to his feet. He's still completely naked. In the morning light, I can now see what yesterday I only felt in the darkness.

Like Dad, he doesn't seem ashamed or abashed in the slightest. His manhood is thick and hard as it lays long against his thigh. When he sees me looking, it bobs outward like an arrow toward me.

Dad hugs me close to his chest and then Dominick comes around to my back. Whereas Dad's hands lift up to caress my jaw, holding me in place while he begins to kiss me deeply, Dominick's hands slip around my waist from behind. Caught so tightly like I am between the two of them, I can feel both of their erections.

Erections.

Holy crap. Dad— He's *hard*. Because of *me*.

And he's kissing me again.

He groans into my mouth and digs his fingers into my scalp like he can't get enough of me. It's early morning but he must not have shaved yet because I can feel the scruff of his beard on my cheek as he drags his mouth to the side to kiss down my throat.

"My sweet girl," he growls low. "I could just eat you up."

From behind me Dominick kisses and suckles at the back of my neck. The sensations of both of their mouths...*oh God*. And Dad, hard through his khaki pants, jabbing at me, it's all so—

And then we're moving. Dad's directing us from the middle of the room sideways.

Toward the bed.

Dominick backs away and lets Dad take control.

Dad never stops kissing me. He lifts me off my feet and carries me the last bit.

He lays me on the bed and follows me down, smoothly landing over me but not crushing me like Dominick did last night.

No, Dad is expert at holding his body right over mine. He pauses kissing me to kneel for a moment to pull his shirt off over his head. His huge chest seems to fill the entire expanse of my vision, the light dusting of blond hair across his strong pectorals with a small trail leading down to his defined abs.

He takes my breath away.

His green eyes pierce mine, watching me watch him. Then, his eyes still locked with mine, he drops his hand and sticks a finger inside me.

"You're so hot for it, aren't you, sweet girl? So creamy and juicy for Daddy."

My sex clenches around his finger and his eyes darken. His member bobs and presses against the top of my thigh.

"So tight," he hisses.

"She's a virgin, Dad," Dominick says. He's joined us on the bed. He arranges himself beside my head and starts to caress my hair back from my face.

Dad sticks another finger inside me. "Fuck," he curses swiftly, his eyes going even wider. He looks wild in a way I've never seen before. Young and unconstrained and gorgeous and terrifying. Yet, still like the Dad I adore.

"You're on the pill, right, baby? I've seen you taking it in the morning."

I nod, swallowing hard. I take it to regulate my period. But, oh my God, does that mean— Does he want to—? Like, *right now*?

Dad grins down at me, looking part angel, part devil. The handsome lines of his face seem to glow in the morning light. He pulls out the two fingers he has inside me and quickly unbuttons his pants, shoving them down and revealing his huge erection.

Larger even than Dominick's. Longer by at least an inch and thicker too.

"Look at me baby. In my eyes." There's a smirk in that last part.

I jerk my attention back to Dad's face. I'm embarrassed he caught me staring but there are way too many other thoughts going through my head for it to last long. Dad's sobered now too.

"It's okay to cry. Remember that, baby," he whispers, leaning down to kiss me. "I'll cherish your tears."

Then I feel him down there. His *thing*.

God, Sarah, you're about to have sex. Call it what it is.

His cock.

I feel it at my entrance, nudging at my lips. He finds what he's looking for.

I expect more exploration.

I expect gentle probing.

A slow push.

Inch by inch.

Instead, Dad commands Dominick, "Hold her shoulders."

Dominick does. And then Dad's battering ram of a cock splits me wide open.

SIX

I scream.

I can't help it.

It hurts.

More than I thought it would.

"Fuck yes," Dad pants, pulling out and then ruthlessly jamming back in.

I holler again and Dad clutches my body to him.

"Dad, slow down!" Dominick shouts, ripping at Dad's shoulder.

But Dad just thrusts even harder. "Let me hear it, baby. Scream for Daddy."

And I do.

I don't know what's happening. I feel like I'm being torn apart. He's so huge. Too big. *Too big.*

And I don't understand the things he's saying.

His voice is... there's still affection there, but it has an edge. Dark, almost mean. And what he's doing—

He pistons in and out of me, just using me. Using me for his pleasure.

Because when I open my eyes, I see his pleasure so clearly on his features. His forehead is scrunched in concentration, his mouth slightly open. I've never seen him look so... raw. Passionate. Still wild. Still gorgeous. But in a barbaric way.

"You're so fucking tight, little girl," he pants. "You're my good girl. You waited for us. What a good girl."

"Dad, stop it," Dominick calls again, "slow down, don't hurt her!"

But Dad's lost in the haze of what he's doing to me. He leans over, I think to kiss me. Instead of landing on my mouth, though, his lips land on my upper cheeks. He's kissing away my tears.

His tongue teases between his lips and then I'm not sure if he's kissing them away so much as tasting them. His movements slow too, though, so that when he next thrusts in, it's a long, languorous stroke.

And for the first time, I don't feel pain, so much as *fullness* when he does it. I gasp instead of grunt in pain and Dad smiles against my cheeks.

"That's right, baby. You feel how big Daddy is inside you? That's Daddy's big cock fucking you so good."

My chest rises and falls and my eyes shoot open as I look up to meet his gaze. His words are so *wrong*. Screwed up beyond belief.

But he looks so lost in the moment as he says it. So lost in *me*. He drops his gaze and looks down our bodies to where he moves in and out of me. In and out.

He squeezes his eyes shut and his entire face knots in pleasure. His pace picks up. "God. *Fuck*. Dom, kiss your sister. I can't take care of her right now. She's too fucking tight. Milking my dick so goddamn good."

Dominick's eyebrows are drawn together in distress. His eyes flick back and forth between my face and Dad's like he's not sure what to do. He caresses my hair and down to my shoulders.

"Shh, it's going to be okay, beautiful," he whispers, sounding both upset and like he's trying to be reassuring. He leans down and drops the softest kiss to the top of my forehead right at my hairline.

In contrast to Dad, who's gone back to driving me into the bed he's plowing my vagina hard, Dominick's kisses are so butterfly soft I can barely feel them at first. His hand comes to my cheek.

"You're doing so good," he whispers, lips brushing back and forth across mine. "I'm so sorry the first time has to hurt. We'll make it feel good now, I promise."

And then he kisses me a little more deeply, but so, so achingly slowly. All the while, his gentle hands come to my body. Tentative hands explore my breasts. Confusing and heartbreaking because he was rough with them last night. Now he caresses and drops down to worship gently with his mouth.

As hard as Dad is, Dominick is all soft.

It's the same when Dominick's hand moves south and he begins teasing at the bud he brought to life earlier even as Dad continues jackhammering in and out just an inch lower.

And always, Dominick's mouth continues its worshipful exploration. Down my neck. Latching onto my nipples.

Dad's dirty tirade never lets up either. Words I've heard before, but pouring from his mouth, they're shocking. Horrifying. Electrifying.

"Never want out of this cunt. Goddamn, gripping me so good. I'm gonna stay in my baby girl forever. Fuuu*u*ck. So fucking good. That's right. Grip Daddy's cock so good. Never gonna stop plowing this tight little pussy."

Dominick's hand on my sex starts circling.

I can't believe the haze of pain has faded enough for pleasure to start rolling through my body again, but it does.

"Fuck, she just clenched so good on my dick when you did that, son," Dad said. "Flip her and get underneath so you can eat her out. I've been wanting to get at that ass again anyway."

Dom's head jerks up at Dad. "Not tonight."

I'm barely aware of what's going on to make out their conversation, much less decipher the meaning of their unspoken words.

"I take what I want when I want," Dad says, eyes narrowing on Dominick. "But fine, we already agreed about the first time."

What are they talking about? They agreed—?

Dominick nods and then before I can even start to—

Dad slips out of me and they easily flip me so I'm facing down on the bed. What now?

"Up on top of Dominick," Dad orders.

"I— What?" I look up helplessly, seeing Dominick laid beside me, but with his feet where my head are. Now that we've stopped for a moment, the panic that I managed to push down ever since it all began is starting to bubble up again.

This is insane. I don't know what I'm doing. I feel like I've fallen down some rough sex-themed Alice and Wonderland.

My body is high and thrumming with need but also sore. I'm confused and I don't know what's going on and—

"Like this," Dominick says, putting his hands on my hips and urging me down the bed. "Come sit on my face, beautiful. I want to make you feel good again."

"I don't know if—"

But my paltry hesitation is ignored as Dominick lifts one of my legs over his chest and settles me upside down on top of him so that his mouth has perfect access to—oh *holy mother of God*.

He sucks just my clitoris into his mouth. Yes, I know the name for it too. I just never even let myself think it or acknowledge it. But, oh hell, Dom sucks my clit so good. He tongues around it and then laps at it till I'm squirming and panting and letting out little whines.

"Fuck, I can't stand those noises," Dad says. "I gotta get back in there."

And then walks around the side of the bed until he's standing behind me. He grabs my hips and then his cock is back. There's only the slightest pinch now and then the fullness. Such fullness while Dominick continues worshipping me with his tongue. When Dad thrusts in, he hits at a different angle than before. So deep it steals my breath.

"Look at that tight little ass."

Smack. Dad's hand comes down hard on my ass cheek. "Fuck, I just want to ride your little virgin ass so hard. Just demolish and fucking desecrate you."

The noise of our bodies—the indecent sex noises of skin slapping against skin, Dad's low, animal grunt every time he bottoms out, my high-pitched whine as Dominick takes me higher. I don't know how much more I can take. I bow my head low on Dominick's abdomen, I'm both exhausted and wired at the same time. His cock bobs up and lays flat on his stomach near my face.

Am I supposed to be doing something with it? Sucking him like he is me?

Oooooooh God. He is making me feel *sooooooo* good. I reach forward and lick the angry red, bulbous tip of his cock, but he moves his hips away from me.

Guess that answers that question. I drop my head back against the hard ridges of his abs and let myself ride higher and higher on the peak of pleasure.

"Do you feel your Daddy fucking you?" Dad asks in almost a shout. "Answer me, little girl. Who's fucking you?"

"You are."

He spanks me hard.

I yelp and buck against Dominick's mouth.

"Who's fucking you?" he shouts again.

Why? Why is he making me say it?

Dominick's mouth pulls back right when I need him to suck. Oh God, just suck harder and send me over the edge already.

I press down against his mouth, his face, but he won't give me what I need.

"My daddy is fucking me," I finally whisper.

Dad leans closer, then bites my ear lobe, not too hard, just enough to sting. "Who is fucking you? Louder!" He jams his cock in deeper than he has yet.

"My daddy is fucking me!"

Dominick latches on to my clit and sucks.

Dad roars and punches his pelvis into me twice more and then he shoves in and holds me so tight, I can feel him shudder and shake.

I cry out as I come along with Dad, him buried deeper than I ever would have thought possible inside me.

One fucked up, entangled-beyond-belief family.

SEVEN

Dad collapses over my back for a moment, breathing heavily, his sweat-slicked forehead bowed against my shoulder blades.

I'm recovering too. Just imagining the erotic image of the three of us horizontally sandwiched like this—Dad's head down on my back, my head and hair spread across Dominick's stomach, his head still between my splayed knees—it's almost enough to have me on the edge of a fresh climax.

Dad's the first to speak. "Sorry, Dominick, I wasn't thinking."

At first I think he's apologizing for crushing Dominick, but as ever, Dad's full of surprises.

"You've got to get in your sister's tight little cunt. Do it now, while she's still wet and fresh."

Dad gets up and helps roll me of Dominick. I stand shakily and look at Dad, eyes wide. Is he serious? My legs feel like jelly and I have to hold onto the bottom of the bedframe so I don't sink to the floor.

Dad cradles my face. "It's a big day for all of us, sweetie. You aren't going to cheat your brother out of having your juicy cunt on the day you lose your virginity, are you? Do you know what a gift that is for a man?"

I blink. Well, when he puts it that way...

Um. I guess...not?

I look over at Dominick.

His eyes are on me. He lifts a hand to cup my face. "You don't have to do anything you don't want to, Sarah."

I glance back at Dad. He doesn't say anything to contradict Dom, but a look of disappointment comes into his eyes at my hesitation.

I take a deep breath and I lift my eyes back to Dominick. "How do you, um...you know...want it?" I gesture back at the bed.

Dominick never got off and he lays down. Then he gestures for me to join him. "Are you sure? I mean it. You don't have to—"

"Don't be a fucking pussy."

Dominick glares at his father but I just reach out and put a hand on his shoulder.

"I want you," I whisper.

His eyes never leave mine. "Then come here, beautiful."

I nod and get back on the bed. As soon as I do, he takes my hand. With the contact, my nervousness immediately flees.

This is my Dominick.

He lifts up and kisses me as he directs me how to sit across his lap.

He pauses again. "You sure?"

My heart leaps at his caution and consideration. So welcome after Dad's callousness.

I nod and put a hand to his cheek. *Yes.* I want this with him. I need it. Everything is a confused jumble, but God, I need this connection with him more than anything right now.

He doesn't take his eyes off me as he lines himself up at my entrance. Unlike Dad, though, he lets me direct the pace as to how fast I want to slide down on him. And his talented fingers are back at work.

The bed squeaks with Dad's weight as he sits down behind me. Dad lifts my hair off my neck and then bites at my ear before whispering, "Oh yeah. What's it feel like having your brother's big cock going in that slick little pussy, sweet girl?"

My sex clenches around the tip of Dominick's cock. The soreness is a little more apparent again, but not bad. Dad's words make me feel strange. Both guilty and turned on. I don't like the confusion they make me feel even as my stomach tightens with arousal.

I continue lowering myself on Dominick. I hiss as he starts to fill me up and lock eyes with him. His eyes are wide with wonder. I clench around him in response. His hands come up to my waist.

At first I worry he's holding me so that he has leverage to jam himself into me really hard like Dad did.

But no, his hands simply caress reverently up and down my ribcage.

"You're so beautiful," Dominick whispers, then he does an ab curl to lift up and kiss me. I sink the last little bit of the way down so that I'm fully impaled.

It's the sweetest moment.

And then Dad starts to pluck at my nipples. "So hot. That's right. Fuck your brother good." Dad sucks at my neck while Dominick kisses me.

Well, at Dad's words, Dominick breaks away for the slightest moment. I think I see his face tighten with some kind of tension, but then his lips are on mine the next second.

Every worry, every thought, every apprehension I've had about everything that's happened throughout the entire morning evaporates under Dominick's kisses. Having him wrapped around me—while also having him inside me? Dad's manhood might might have the slightest physical edge on Dom, but I've never felt more *full* than when I'm with Dominick in this way.

Full of love. Full of warmth. Safety. Safe-keeping.

When he finally starts moving his shaft in and out, it's the most *right* thing in the world. Almost instantly, I'm on the edge of climax

Dominick sees it.

Of course he does. He's sitting up so that we're chest to chest, still holding me close though I can't imagine the abdominal strength it must be taking for him to keep the position. He swivels his hips up and into me, hitting me at such a perfect angle.

Dad bites the back of my neck, but I barely feel it because *Dominick*—and then waves and waves of—*ohhhhhhh*.

Where the other orgasms today were sharp and short, this one is a warm heat that lights me up from my core. It washes outward to the tips of my fingers and then flows through every follicle of hair. No corner or cell or molecule of my body is left untouched. I gasp with the shock and pleasure and how fully Dominick just penetrated every single bit of my being.

I've never felt so beautiful, so—

"Look at our little whore, son," Dad says, pinching my nipples hard. "Little nympho just milked your cock like she lives for it. God, they always want it so bad."

I yank away from Dominick, mortified, and swing around to look at his dad.

What a jerk! What just happened between Dominick and I was so perfect and he—

"How did it feel to have both your Daddy and your brother's cocks inside you within half an hour, sweet girl?" Dad's voice is softer as he cups my cheek. With his other hand, he's yanking roughly at his cock. He's fully erect again, and he twists when he gets to the glistening tip, then jams his hand back down.

My tirade dies on my lips.

Oh my God, he's right. I just let two different men have sex with me, one right after the other. If that's not the very definition of a whore, what is?

Dominick slips out of me and Dad's hand slides around to grab my hair. Dad gets on his knees on the bed and he pushes me down on my back.

"Open your mouth. Swallow what Daddy gives you. Show me how much you love being a little whore for Daddy."

Then he starts jacking himself off right over my face.

Just like they did in that one porno my friend Bonny made me watch one time. I thought it was degrading and horrible then.

And now? I don't know. I don't know. It's happening and I can't think—

"Open up," Dad commands, slapping my cheek with his dick, his face going dark when my mouth remains closed. "Don't make Daddy punish you again."

Desperately, I search for Dominick. He's sitting on the other side of the bed, his back to us.

"Dominick," I whisper.

Dominick turns to me immediately. I reach out a hand and he takes it. I open my mouth to say something else and cum hits my face.

"Sweet little whore!" Dad shouts.

I sputter as cum fills my mouth and coats my cheeks. My eyes squeeze shut so I'm not prepared when the cock shoves in my mouth.

"Suck it," Dad orders. "Suck it clean."

"Dad!" Dominick objects, but I do what I'm told.

I open wide and accept the big, thick object in. The cum is strange tasting, salty and bitter and a little sour. I lick and suck and cough and I'm pretty sure there are tears running down my cheeks, mixing with the mess.

Dad finally pulls his cock out of my mouth. He brings his large hand to my face. With his thumb, he rubs my cheek, smearing my tears together with the remainder of his cum. "My sweet, sweet girl," he murmurs before kissing the top of my head and then dropping to the side of me. He reaches for a pillow, one of which somehow managed to actually stay on the bed in spite of... all of it.

He shoves it underneath his head and closes his eyes. He looks perfectly at peace. His chest and temples are sweat-slicked, sure, but he seems like he just finished a vigorous workout. Worn out but like he has no worries in the world.

Certainly not like he just finished deflowering his step-daughter along with his son in an insane threesome.

I'm afraid to look in Dominick's direction.

If he's fallen asleep just as easily and left me alone, after—

After—

I open my mouth and try to take a breath but the air just isn't there. And there's still Dad's cum all over me. I gasp for air again but still can't manage it.

"Sarah, come on."

Once again, Dominick's strong hand grasps mine.

That air I was searching for so desperately finally flows into my lungs. I look over at Dom and his hazel eyes are full of concern. He helps me off the bed. It's warm in the house but my body is covered in goosebumps. I shiver as he leads me out of my room.

I have no idea where he's taking me but I feel less and less connected to my body or my life or really… anything at the moment.

Is this what every girl feels like after losing her virginity?

Is this what it means to transition to womanhood? Like you dissociate from your own body for a little bit and feel kind of floaty and weird and—

"Sarah? You okay? You still with me?"

"Huh?" I look over at Dominick as he leads me into his room and closes the door behind us. Dominick's eyebrows furrow and his mouth tightens.

"Christ, Sarah." He wets a wash cloth under warm water from the sink and gently scrubs at my face. And then he pulls me into his chest and wraps his arms around me.

For a second I'm sure this is the start of the next round and I tense up. I wait for his hands to drop to my bottom. Or for him to grip my hair and jerk my head back.

But he just…holds me.

Hugging me.

He's hugging me.

When he tries to pull back, I cling tighter.

"Sarah honey, I'm not letting you go." He whispers into my hair. "But we need to get you in the bath. You're freezing. And I can just imagine how sore you must be." He winces and his face crumbles. "I want to make it better. Please let me make it better."

His words. They open the dam I didn't even know I was holding back inside me. A sob bubbles up and I press my head even harder against his warm chest as he leads me to his ensuite bathroom.

He puts a hand on the back of my head and holds me to him while we walk. "Shhhh, shhhh," he whispers. "It's all going to be okay. It'll be okay. I promise. I'll make it okay. I swear."

When he tries to pull away from me to turn on the bath faucet, I don't let him. The first burst of tears has slowed, but I can't, I just can't release him yet.

He finally maneuvers us so that he can get to the faucet with me attached to him like a starfish suckered to the front of his body.

The splash of the water against the porcelain tub as it fills up is the only sound for a little while. I like the soothing noise it makes. And when I snuggle a little further to the right, the steady thump of Dominick's heart calms me down even more. I'm so cold and he's so warm. I want him to keep me warm forever.

The water finally stops.

"It's ready," Dominick says. "You've gotta let go so I can help you in."

I shake my head against his chest. "I'll be fine. I don't need a bath." I hold him even tighter.

After a second, he sighs, then says, "Okay, let go of your death grip and we'll go in together. Deal?"

I look up at him and smile.

His eyebrows are still slanted in concern, but at my smile, his face softens.

His eyes search mine.

"I love you," he whispers.

And my heart explodes.

That's a thing, it really is. And it's what happens to my heart. Just like earlier, when my orgasm reached throughout my entire body—his words do that now.

Because I feel the same way.

Today has been full of confusion and madness and pleasure and pain but finally here is something I *know* to be true—I love Dominick Winters.

His eyes widen and he claps his hand over my mouth. "Don't say it back. I mean— You don't have to say it back. I mean Christ," he shakes his head, his neck reddening. "I don't expect you to feel the same yet. Or ever," he rushes on. "I would never try to pressure you. And after today..." His eyes shoot back in the direction of my room and his face clouds over.

Meanwhile, I reach up and pull at his hand on my mouth. He finally seems to notice me yanking at him.

"Sorry," he says and drops his hand.

I can't contain it another second. "I—"

"Don't—" He cuts me off, this time just with a finger over my lips. "Please, promise you won't say anything about what I just said. Swear you won't. I can't bear it, okay?"

"But—"

He shakes his head vehemently. "Swear."

I look up at him unhappily but finally nod my head. Why won't he let me share my feelings with him? Is he afraid I'll say I *don't* love him or that I'll say I *do*? Is he regretting what he said already? Did he not mean it, is that it? And if he does love me, why wouldn't he want to hear it back?

"Come on," he smiles at me again and kisses the tip of my nose. "Let's get in before the water gets cold." And with that, he lifts a foot into the bath.

I follow him. He settles me in front of him in the bath. The hot water feels good but stings slightly against my sore sex.

The soothing warmth and Dominick behind me soon make all the worries of the day slip away, though.

"You know I'll always take care of you, don't you, beautiful?" he whispers into my hair, wrapping his arms around me and pulling me close.

I nod drowsily and settle my back against his chest.

He chuckles into my hair. "Rest. You deserve it."

The world dissolves into the warmth and the comfort I feel in his arms. I'm not sure if his next words are real or I just imagine them. "I love you. I'll never let you be hurt again. I swear, Sarah. I swear on my life."

EIGHT

If you would have told me that after a torrid threesome with my stepfather and stepbrother, life would go on as usual, I would never have believed it.

People who've had *sex* with each other can't be...*normal*...around each other. Especially after the darker side of Dad I saw come out.

But when we get out of the bath, we find that Dad's been called in to work. The next week is an especially busy one and I barely see either of the boys except at family dinner each night.

Monday I prepare enchiladas and am ready for everything to be super weird between us all. I was wired about it all day through my classes. Not to mention that sitting through said classes was not especially pleasant because losing one's virginity—especially in such a... *vigorous* fashion...*God, just say it like it is, Sarah*: two Viking-like men fucked your brains out. And it's left me sore as hell.

But when Dad comes in at six-fifteen on the dot, he says hi and goes up to shower like nothing at all is unusual.

I'm left thinking maybe I just imagined the whole thing? But nope, the soreness between my legs can attest that I did *not* just have a very vivid fantasy over the weekend.

I felt like Dominick was a bit more wary when he got home after working back to back Sunday-Monday shifts. He kept watching me like I was fine china that might break at any moment when he came in, offering to get things out of the oven, set the table, make tea.

I finally snapped at him to take his seat and get out of my kitchen. He did and then everything was normal. Well, apart from Dad coming in after his shower and smacking my ass before sitting down. "Smells great, sweet girl."

But that was that. We talked about our days just like normal and no other references were made to our torrid Saturday session.

The whole week's been like that.

It's Thursday and I don't know whether to continue being antsy or if it's been so long, lowering my guard is okay.

And lowering my guard against what, exactly?

I love Dominick.

And Dad?

Initially when they first moved in, he was the one I connected to more.

I bite my lip as I strain the pasta and then put it back in the pot with the alfredo sauce. But now, my feelings for Dad are more complicated.

I think it's just that I was so unprepared for what happened on Saturday. It came out of left field. I didn't know what was going to come next or was expected of me. And then Dad was so...

I blink hard and stir the alfredo sauce as I glance out the kitchen window. It's a picturesque view into the tree lined street. The sun has set and it's getting dark. A fat squirrel runs up the limb of the ancient oak that shades our townhouse. I smile as another squirrel chases it around and around.

"What are you dreaming about, sweet girl?"

I screech and twirl around so quickly, the spoon I was stirring the sauce with goes flying. "Oh God, you scared me," I wheeze, then smack at Dad's shoulder.

He grins and makes a fake pained expression at my blow.

"Oh no, I made you spill. Sorry, sweetie." He kisses the top of my head and moves to grab a paper towel to clean up the small spray of sauce that trails the counter and floor. He picks up the spoon and tosses it in the sink.

My heart melts a little in my chest. This is the kind man I first welcomed into my home and my heart. Is it possible to make space for both Dominick *and* Dad?

God, is that even...okay?

Or is it sick and twisted?

Everything I was ever taught growing up says *yes*, all of this is completely screwed up. FUBAR as my first boyfriend would have put it.

Beyond *all* repair.

But Dominick didn't seem to think so. He just took it in stride when Dad joined in. This is normal for them.

And they're my family. Family. Something I've never had before and always wanted. You make compromises for family. You stretch and grow for them.

Haha. Well, Dad certainly *stretched* me last Saturday.

Um. Okay, now I'm making really FUBAR jokes in my head.

"I'll set the table," I say, shaking my head, completely disturbed at the whole situation. I still no idea which way is up or down.

"Is Dominick going to make it tonight?" I ask.

"Nope, it's just the two of us."

My heart thumps harder.

But then Dad and I have a perfectly normal dinner. He talks about the extension for the oncology wing he and the board have been working on for a couple years now. Fundraising is always both the nightmare and lifeblood of Dad's work.

"But at least I finally get to enjoy one of the perks."

"What do you mean?" I ask, spearing some spinach from my salad and then mixing it with a little bit of alfredo. The meal has been so relaxing, I'm almost finished with my plate. When I'm nervous or uptight, I can barely eat a thing. But Dad's so charismatic, I have the feeling he could make the Pope feel at ease in a stripclub.

He smiles as he dishes out a second serving of pasta for himself. "There's a Father-Daughter Dance and Fundraiser this weekend for donors. Of course the hospital higher-ups such as yours truly are expected to attend." He puts down his fork, his green eyes earnest. "It'd be an honor if you'd go with me."

For a second, there's a lump in my throat. It's so stupid, I know it is.

But there are just certain things you miss out on when you don't have a dad around growing up. All things dad-related—it's just impossible not to feel cut out from a lot when you're a kid. Take Your Daughter to Work Day. Innocuous teacher questions like, *what do your parents do?* The country club Father-Daughter Dance all my friends went to when I was thirteen—yes, when you run in the circles my family does, you're supposed to attend pretentious things like that. All of it just put a spotlight on the glaring hole in my life.

And when I asked Mom where my real dad was and why he left?

I only got cursing, inevitably followed by days of binge drinking even worse than normal. I asked Grandpa once and was told my father was a lowlife scum who would never get a cent of the family fortune. So that was that.

But here's this man now eager to step into the role. Gorgeous and vibrant. He wants me. In every sense of the word.

Dad.

I beam at him even as my stomach twists with the knowledge that this is screwed up. And I'm screwed up for wanting it. Really screwed up for wanting it as much as I do.

"I can't wait." The words are off my lips before I can even think them through.

Dad reaches over and squeezes my hand. His grin stretches across his face. I've made him so happy.

How can that be wrong?

We sit there, eyes and hands locked for a moment, then Dad lets go and we return to eating. He asks me about classes and dinner continues as normal.

After dinner, I do the dishes and Dad dries. Dad finally puts the last dish away. Then he gives my shoulder a squeeze and kisses the back of my head. "Sleep tight, sweet girl."

I turn and watch his back as he disappears out the kitchen door.

Then I shake my head and brace my hands against the kitchen counter.

Six months ago I would have been eating ramen while buried in blankets on my bed, watching endless reality TV and wishing my life was even half so interesting as it is now. Often crying myself to sleep from loneliness and hoping for something—*anything*—to change.

And now I have the attention and affection of not one but *two* men.

Maybe I should stop worrying and complaining and just...you know, try to enjoy it.

Whoa, what a shocking thought.

Me, actually enjoying my life and not just doing what I'm supposed to do like a good little autobot? Perish the thought!

God, I've lived so long in fear of repeating Mom's mistakes that I've barely allowed myself to even *live*. Never color outside the lines, Sarah. Do the dishes and clean up after your slob of a mother, Sarah. Never let anyone see what a screwed up homelife you have, Sarah.

Look perfect.

Be perfect.

But... what if I just gave it all up?

All the self-judgement.

All the guilt at stepping a toe outside the line.

What if I let go of shame?

Let go of everything and learn who *Sarah* really is apart from my mother's daughter? Completely unshackled?

Just the idea releases the heaviness that's been weighing me down ever since last weekend. Then I immediately feel exactly how exhausted I am.

I've barely been sleeping. Every night waiting for something, I don't even know what—one or both of them to show up at my door. I shake my head and laugh at myself.

Whatever this is, I'm sure we can sit down like mature adults and discuss it and what we want it to be. I don't know why I've been so wimpy about it. I've let fear rule me for too long. I should have spoken up and asked more questions on Saturday. Clarified exactly what was going on, what I was confused about, and what I wanted.

Communication. You know, that little thing everyone talks about as the most important element in any relationship? How are the guys supposed to know what I want unless I speak up? I want to smack my forehead at how obvious the solution to all my anxiety is.

I put the dish sponges up to dry and hurry up the stairs to my room, feeling much lighter than I have all week. Taking a shower only further loosens the last little bit of tension from my muscles. I slip into bed, totally calm and relaxed.

I settle under the covers and read for a while until it's nine-thirty and my eyes get too heavy to stay open any more. It's early for me but after my week of non-sleep, I turn off my overhead light and slip back into bed.

My nightlight's on. Naturally.

Just the perfect level of darkness. I close my eyes and settle onto my side. I'm about to doze off when I get the slightest chill down my spine. Silly, but I think it's because my back is to the door.

Which is absolutely ridiculous. Oh my God, what am I? Seven years old?

Still, I roll over, open my eyes quickly, see that my door is firmly shut, and breathe out in relief.

Then I close my eyes again and snuggle deeper into my pillow.

Still, a second later, that same stupid chill comes again.

I internally roll my eyes at myself and groan. I refuse to spend another sleepless night jumping at every other noise.

Still, I obey the dumb compulsion and my eyes flip open.

Only to see Dad's huge silhouette filling my door.

I scream and grab my pillow to my chest. Then I throw it at him. "You scared the crap out of me."

Dad catches the pillow, chuckling as he steps into the room and approaches my bed. "Daddy's sorry, sweet girl." His voice seems deeper than it was just a couple of hours ago in the kitchen.

In only a few of his long-legged strides, he's over to my bedside. He sits down and lays his large hands on my shoulders. Without much effort he rolls me slightly so that I'm on my stomach and he's massaging my back.

"You've told me about your homework and what you've been doing at school during dinner the past few days," Dad says, leaning over, "but you haven't told me what I've really wanted to know." This last part he hisses in my ear.

I tremble underneath him as his hands get rougher kneading my shoulder muscles and the back of my neck.

"W-w-what's that?" I ask, hating how timid my voice sounds. Why am I muttering like a bumbling idiot. I'm supposed to be communicating my wants and needs. I take a gulp of air. "I was hoping we could talk tonight ab—"

"You haven't told me whether or not you've been a good girl or a bad girl," he growls. And then without waiting for me to reply, he flips me over on his lap, yanks down my panties, and his palm lands on my ass.

I yelp in surprise as he spanks me again, hard and sure. "Have you been letting other boys look at what's mine?" he asks before landing another smack. "Have you been flaunting that tight little ass and making the schoolboys' cocks hard now that you know how good dicks feel shoved up your nasty cunt?"

"Wha—? No, I would nev—"

"Don't lie to me!" he yells. "Once little girls get cock, it's all they can think about. I know how you little sluts are. I try to find you when you're pure. Before the world corrupts you. When you're still sweet. Are you still my sweet girl?"

He jams a finger up inside me.

And I'm not dry.

I'm slick. As rough as he is, his finger slips right in.

Somehow all of his rough, filthy talk, even his meanness, has made me wet.

I *like* this?

This turns me on?

Dad sticks a second finger inside me and starts to scissor them, stretching me and making me even slicker for him.

"Fuck but you're so sweet and tight while you're still innocent," he mumbles into my hair. "You smell like a beautiful, sweet little girl should. So clean and fresh and good."

"Just for you and Dom," I whisper, panting and on the edge of tears again even while confusing sensations of pleasure rise up in my belly. "No one else. Ever!"

I don't know why he's saying the things he's saying. They're mean and hurtful and I was supposed to be standing up for myself. Talking in a mature way about what I want and expect and—

"Christ, sweet girl, maybe you *are* the one after all," Dad says.

Then he flips me over and I hear the noise of a buckle being undone.

Even though I'm expecting it, the brief second of bracing myself still isn't enough to prepare for his giant cock breaching me.

There's no gentle nudge and exploration of my lips like Dominick did. No, like before, Dad impales me long and hard, piercing me straight through and pinning me to the bed.

I let out a low, "*oof*," at the pain of it.

It's such a tight fit, that even though I'm no longer a virgin and was wet—God there's no denying it still hurts. Not nearly as much as the first time. But he's still just too damn *big*. And I was wet, but not *that* wet.

He groans low with the first stick, then almost immediately pulls out and shoves back in.

The sting makes it impossible to feel any pleasure. I'm sure my face is a grimace, but Dad just cups my cheeks. "You're doing so good, sweet girl. You're making Daddy feel so good. do you have any idea what a good girl you are? You let Daddy fuck you so good."

Then he kisses me.

His kisses are nothing like Dominick's kisses. Dad kisses just like he screws. His tongue is forceful. Thrusting. He pulls back to kiss my lips but only because he's half-nipping and biting. Always with teeth. Never for a second am I allowed any leeway in the kiss. He's in command every second.

I'm left gasping and confused.

Right when the pain starts to ebb and the pleasure starts to warm in my center again, Dad pulls out. He lifts me off the bed. I stumble to my feet but Dad's sharp voice commands, "On your knees."

I get on my knees on the hard floor. I'm off-kilter. Like before, everything's a haze. There's only Dad. This moment. His voice.

"Open."

I don't— What does he—

His hands are on my jaw when I don't respond quickly enough, urging my jaw open.

Oh, he means—

He's shoving his cock in my mouth before I even finish the thought. He jams it to the back of my throat and beyond.

"Swallow it," he orders.

I try to protest that I can't. I don't know. *I don't—* None of this is —I can't—

He just pulls out and pushes his cock past my lips and into my throat, choking me again.

"Godfuckingdammit," he yells. "That's right, gag on Daddy's giant cock. Do you know how much I love that sound?" he asks, all but a shout. "Your innocent fucking noises drive me fucking crazy. Gag on me again," he shoves it in and I'm gagging, choking, spitting. Oh God, I'm going to die if he keeps it up much longer.

"*Fuuuuuuuuuuuck*," he yells and with one more gagging thrust his cum is spurting into my mouth and spilling down onto my cheeks and chin to my chest.

"Swallow," he pants. "Swallow it now or I'll punish you so hard you won't sit for a week!"

I gag and try but I just keep spitting and sputtering.

Then he reaches down and pinches my nose shut. Can't breathe! Can't—! Why would he—?

"Swallow!" he roars again.

But in all my panicking, I do swallow.

And when I do, it's like a switch flips.

I swallow and gasp and lick at everything covering my lips. And then I suckle at Daddy's cock and lick every drop from his fingers when he gathers a puddle of it from my breast and shoves it in my mouth. I have to please Daddy. I'll do anything to please Daddy.

In the end, Daddy's beaming at me, a halo behind him from my nightlight.

"You might just be Daddy's perfect little girl after all. Don't wash up until morning."

He leaves me there just like that, heaving for breath and totally destroyed, his cum still all over me, inside and out.

NINE

I walk through school the next day in an absolute daze.

When my Early Childhood Development group leader asks me if everything's okay, I just nod and walk away without saying anything. Usually she's the closest thing to a friend I have at school and whenever we talk I try to leverage it into going to grab coffee. Today I literally just walk away. As if she's a wooden post. I pretend I don't hear her even though she was standing right in front of my face.

"Sarah?" she calls after me.

I keep walking across the quad.

Part of my mind keeps trying to force me to face what happened last night.

But the rest is sane and keeps bricking up new walls and throwing away the key as quickly as that pesky little concerned part knocks down the old ones.

Nothing happened last night.

I did not become some pathetic sex slave who humiliated herself in order to please her Daddy.

Because that is *not* who I am.

Not that I actually know who I am.

Nineteen, almost twenty, years on this planet and I haven't managed to figure that out yet. I thought I could start figuring it out, but *nope*. That didn't happen.

It's just fucking pathetic no matter how you look at it.

So I won't.

Look at it, that is.

None of it.

Self-examination is *so* overrated.

I will live in the moment.

And not think.

Thinking about shit is where the problem is.

And I cuss now.

That's a new thing I do.

Because fuck it.

Fuck. All. Of. It.

Not that I'm thinking about it.

Whatever *it* might be.

Goddamn motherfucking shit.

Can someone please just give me an escape pod from my head?????

"Sarah. Thank God. I've been looking everywhere for you."

I jerk to a stop right outside of the Student Commons and look to my left.

"Dominick?"

Okay, maybe I'm really out of it, but I could swear Dominick is jogging my way across the quad. I blink hard. But yeah, it still looks like Dominick—decked out like always in his blue scrubs with the black Henley underneath, the strap of the leather carrier bag he always takes with him slung diagonally across his chest.

"Sarah." Dom catches up to me and immediately envelops me in a hug.

I don't respond at first. Even with his arms around me, the fog persists.

"Sarah?" He pulls back and shakes my shoulders slightly.

"Sarah?" The worry in his voice is the only thing that finally pierces through the haze. "Are you all right?" he asks.

Then he pulls me back into his arms. "Christ, it's obvious you aren't."

"No, I'm fine," I mutter, blinking.

Dominick's here. On my campus. How is he here? How is this possible?

"What are you doing here—?"

"I had to see you," he cuts me off, his hand on the back of my head, pressing me even more firmly into his chest. "Dad wasn't supposed to go to your room last night. He said he wouldn't go without me. I came as soon as I heard he did. I'm so sorry if he scared you."

As soon as he says the words, my whole body starts to tremble. It's like him saying it out loud has finally given me permission to feel it.

Fear.

Yes. That's exactly what I felt last night. I was too confused to even know what to call it. But the whole thing was terrifying. I was afraid.

But I was also turned on by it all. I was wet. So I...liked it. That meant I wanted it... Right?

I press my face into Dominick's chest. I'm still so confused.

But everything feels better in his arms.

The tilting world seems to settle back on its axis.

Impulsively, I reach up on tiptoes and kiss him.

I open my mouth to him, but Dominick surprises me. He pulls back.

Crap.

That was the wrong thing to do—trying to kiss him when he just came here to check on me. Besides, Dad said we aren't supposed to sneak around anymore. Technically, kissing Dom isn't *sneaking around*, but it could be construed that way and—

Then Dominick's lips land on mine and all my thoughts still again.

Blessed quiet in my head.

Dom's tongue doesn't seek entrance and he doesn't press for more. It's just a gentle, sweet, soft press of his lips. And that's it.

After a short moment, he pulls back. Then he leans his forehead against mine.

And I don't care if anyone sees us and makes the connection that he's my new stepbrother. I barely talk to anyone on campus anyway. Having him so close is everything.

"God I've missed you," he whispers, his eyes slipping closed. "These shifts at the hospital have been hell, knowing I'm not keeping my promise of protecting you."

I frown. "Protecting?"

The line between his eyebrow deepens but then he opens his eyes and he smiles at me.

"But I'm here with you now. Come on." He looks around us at students streaming past and the general commotion of the quad. "Let's get out of here and go somewhere quieter."

I nod. I have a class in an hour, but with how little I was able to focus on my morning lectures, nothing sounds better than skipping and spending time with Dominick.

"Do you want to get some coffee or something to eat?" I touch his arm, noting the dark circles under his eyes. "I can only imagine how exhausted you must be. Have you been eating? You've got to remember to take care of yourself, not just your patients, Dom."

His smile widens and his eyes soften as he looks over at me. Then he does the last thing I expect. He reaches over and intertwines his fingers with mine.

Oh my God, he's holding my hand.

Such a simple gesture.

After all the things we did last Saturday, it should feel like the least intimate thing in the world. And yet it makes my heart sing in a way that all the erotic and sexual things I experienced in that room and with his father last night pale in comparison.

"First of all, I want you to know that what happened last night won't happen again. Not without me there." He looks up at me, eyes widening as he rushes on, "And only if you want it to." Then he breathes out and looks down, grimacing like he'd practiced some speech but it came out wrong. "How are you? With everything that's happened? Just say the word and it all stops." He swings our arms back and forth slightly as we walk. I think he's leading us toward a small coffee shop on the corner, but I'm not sure.

And I can't help stiffening at his questions.

He notices.

Of course he notices.

He stops in his tracks at the edge of the quad underneath a blooming cherry tree. "Sarah?"

I shrug, then nod towards the little shop. "Let's get coffee. I need a caffeine fix." I paste on a smile and then tug him across the road as the walk sign starts to flash a countdown.

He lets it go and we go get our coffees. He orders me a white mocha macchiato, my favorite drink when I'm disregarding calories. Which apparently I am today. I don't mind because frankly, I won't deny I'm in need of comfort food. I don't balk at the blueberry scone he buys me either, but only because he gets one for himself too.

It's only after we're out of the coffeeshop and walking down the sidewalk sipping our drinks that Dominick starts up again. "So? Spill."

"What?" I try to deflect, using a stir stick to eat some of the whip cream off the top of my macchiato. Dominick's holding the bag with the scones. I get all the cream and then pop the top back on to drink the rest of the coffee. *God*, that hits the spot.

He lets me avoid his questions a little longer, leading the way to a small park another block and a half down. Then we settle underneath a big tree. I'm not sure what kind, but it has a huge trunk and root system that sticks out of the ground. Dominick takes off his bag and settles himself on one of the roots, back against the trunk. He pats his lap for me to sit.

It's a spring day. Flowers are in bloom. The sun shines bright and happy. The most handsome man I can possibly imagine is gesturing for me to sit with him under a shaded tree with sweet treats awaiting me in a pastry bag.

...And all I feel like doing is curling up against him and crying.

Damn it, what is *wrong* with me?

I bite back the tears as I sit on his knee, set down my coffee on the ground, and snuggle against him.

"Um, you're not allowed to be this perfect," I whisper against his chest, wiping at a stray tear that manages to escape my eye.

He winces underneath me. "God, don't say that." His voice is dark. Full of...self-loathing? I look up at him in confusion.

But his facial features match what I thought I heard in his voice. His mouth is clenched and eyes cast down as he looks away from me.

"Dom? What's wrong."

When he looks up at me, his eyebrows are dropped low. Sorrowful. "Sarah, have you ever stopped to think that maybe my dad isn't the best guy in the world?"

I sit up straighter and look at him. Really look at him.

"But..." I shake my head. "The two of you are so close. I don't understand. I thought you looked up to him. It's why you went into medicine."

He breathes out hard and looks away again. "Things between me and Dad are complicated. I hated him for a long time growing up. I thought he was a monster. That he drove Mom away. But then things changed."

He takes a long drink of his coffee—straight espresso, naturally—before putting down his cup beside mine.

"How? What happened?"

His expression goes dark again. Brow furrowed, dark eyes stormy. He shrugs. "Some stuff went down. I don't really want to get into it. I got really competitive with him. I did some things I'm not proud of. Anyway, all of it convinced me that maybe we weren't that different after all. Like father, like son, ya know?"

His eyes lift briefly to meet mine before he drops them again. "So

I thought, who am I to judge him? Maybe this is just how all people are? Good and bad. Light and dark. We're all just a little screwed up. I sort of accepted it."

He looks up at me again, and this time his eyes are earnest. "So yeah, at first going into medicine was part of the competitive thing. I was going to be a doctor, but be better than he ever was. I would be a surgeon and do a specialty far more impressive than his. I would be one of the best in the country."

He reaches out and grasps my hand again. Like he's desperate for even more of a connection with me than our bodies touching where I sit on his lap. "But I swear it became more than that. It wasn't until I started my residency about a year ago. But when I started interacting with real patients. Seeing the impact of medicine on human lives. Families. Seeing how loved ones rallied around the sick person. Celebrated." Pain knits his brow. "And how they grieved when we lost someone. It all became real. Even if I hadn't started out with the right intentions, I knew that now *this* was why I was going to be in it for the long haul. The patients."

"Oh Dominick," I reach out a hand and cup his cheek. I hate that he feels like he has to plead for me to believe him when anyone can see he cares about his patients *so* much he works himself to the bone. He wants the Boston General residency because he knows it will make him the best doctor, able to save the most lives.

"I know your heart." My hand slides down from his cheek and I settle it over his chest. His heartbeat is steady underneath my palm.

To my bewilderment, his face crumbles at my pronouncement. His head falls forward and he buries his forehead against my breast. "I don't deserve you," he whispers. "Neither of us deserve you."

"Shh, stop it," I move so that I'm straddling him, then I run my fingers through his long, soft hair. I don't care if the position is slightly indecent with me wearing a dress—the bottom has a big round skirt and I'm still perfectly covered.

Besides, all I can think about is Dominick. I just need to get as close to him as possible. I don't know where all this self-denigration is coming from, but I hate it.

The fact that he's opening up to me? That I welcome. I just hate that this is what he's been hiding in his heart. I draw him closer and kiss the top of his head, right where the swirl of his cowlick begins.

"You're going to be just fine," I whisper, looking around at the beautiful spring afternoon. "Both of us are going to be just fine."

And being here in his arms, it feels true. I've felt so lost all day, but he brought me back to myself. It's true that I haven't fully figured out who I am yet... but maybe that's not something to be scared of. Maybe it's something to be excited about.

I get to discover myself. How amazing is that?

And when I'm with Dominick it's like the entire horizon opens up, huge and vast. Full of unending possibilities and a hundred different paths, each with a bright future.

Always with him by my side.

I lean my cheek on top of his head. He pulls me back against the tree and we hold fast to one another.

Finally, I can't keep it inside any more. Without really thinking it through, it just pops out.

"I love you."

The only signal that he hears is his fingers clutch tighter on my waist. Then, for a couple of minutes, nothing. He just keeps holding me, his head buried in my chest.

Except...well, that's not exactly true.

It's after about thirty seconds that I begin to feel it.

I'm straddling him and where my sex is pressed up against his, I start to feel him through his scrubs. His cock becomes noticeably hard, pressing up through the denim and against the thin barrier of my cotton panties.

My breath hitches and unwittingly, my fingers in his hair claw at his scalp.

That only makes his cock jump and harden more.

"Sarah." My name is a long, drawn out groan.

Then he shifts me against him, back and forth, no doubt seeking friction.

The moisture that had just begun to gather becomes a flood at the needy gesture.

Then he stops and breathes out hard, looking up. "Beautiful, no, I don't want to take advantage—"

I scoff. "I'm not a kid." Then I feel my cheeks heat. I know we play at the whole *Daddy* thing but it doesn't mean that I'm actually—

"I know you're not," he hurries to say, obviously reading the expression on my face. And then he kisses me.

Which is the best thing of all.

At least until a couple of catcalls and whistles break out nearby.

I pull away in embarrassment and Dominick helps me to my feet. He shields me from on-lookers while I grab our coffees and pastries. He slings his bag back over his chest.

As soon as we're out of the park, I bust up laughing, covering my mouth with my forearm. Dominick looks down at me like he was afraid of how I might react, but then he starts laughing too.

He tosses our empty coffee cups in a trashcan as we pass. Then he grabs me up in his arms and swings me in a circle. I shriek as he twirls me around once and then twice.

"God, I love you," he says, grinning at me once I'm finally settled on solid ground, still giggling my head off.

The giggles immediately die off. And like two polarized magnets, our lips immediately lock together again.

I can't get enough of him. My legs entwine with his. I need to get closer. I don't care that people are watching. I don't care that we get catcalled again.

"Dominick," I whisper desperately into his mouth between kisses. "Oh God, Dom."

My breathy words seem to break him out of some kind of trance though, because he moves away from me and grabs my hand.

It's not a sweet intertwining of fingers like before.

No, he takes my hand firmly as he urges me forward. Straight down the block in the direction we came from. Back toward the college.

"Where are we—?" But he takes off at a jog to get across the street before the light turns and I hurry to keep up with him.

Before I know it, he's leading me into the towering university library and pressing the button for the elevator. It's mid-afternoon and most students are in class, so for once, there's no one else waiting. As soon as the elevator pings and the doors open, Dominick drags me inside. As soon as the doors close and he's hit the button for the eighth floor, he has me up against the wall and is devouring my mouth again.

When he shoves his leg between my thighs, all I can think is, oh God, *yes*.

It's an older building and the elevator is slow. When Dominick's hands come underneath my buttocks and he hikes me even further up his thigh, I wrap my legs around his waist and flex back and forth for as much friction as I can get.

"Oh God," I breathe out. "Oh Dom."

"I go by either name, beautiful," he says, grinning devilishly and only pulling away when the elevator pings again at the eighth floor.

I'm flushed and so amped by the time he pulls me toward wherever he's taking us, I'm sure that I'd follow this man to hell and back. God or devil, I don't really care right now. I just need him between my thighs again. As soon as possible.

I don't have to wait long. Still gripping my hand, he pulls me down through several racks to a handicapped unisex bathroom. We slip inside and a second later, Dominick's flipped the lock and has me up against the wall.

His hand immediately slips underneath my dress.

My gasp of pleasure echoes throughout the small tiled bathroom and Dominick's other hand lifts a finger to my lips. "Shh," he grins at me. "It's a library, beautiful. Gotta be quiet."

And then the bastard drops to his knees and his head disappears underneath my dress. My panties are at my ankles the next moment and—

Oh sweet Jesus—

I can't help the little moan that escapes my throat. What he's doing with his tongue— Oh God, that should be illegal in all fifty states. Except no, because it feels *sooooooooooooo* good.

After the next high-pitched noise, he lifts the skirt of my dress and gives me a warning look. I slap my own hand over my mouth. If only so he'll get back to it.

He gives me a grin. A very naughty, naughty grin.

And then that wicked, delicious, sent-from-heaven tongue starts to suck, and twist and thrust—

I'm right on the edge when Dominick retreats again, pulling out from underneath my dress and wiping his mouth with his forearm.

What? He can't stop now. I was *thiiiiiiis close* to coming. I reach for him to drag him back but he steps away.

He smirks. "Do you want something?"

I breathe out in frustration. He knows exactly how close I was. I fight hard not to stomp my foot in frustration. Then again, I *did* say I wasn't a child.

But it's not *fair!*

"Come here and you can get your treat," he says with a clear teasing note in his voice. He leans over and grabs something I can't see from his bag.

"What is that?" I step forward to try to look over his shoulder.

"Ah ah ah," he chides, moving whatever it is out of my sight. He looks back at me and gestures toward the sink. "Assume the position like a good little girl."

I look at the sink and then back at him. Does he mean like when…?

"Hands on the counter, ass out," he confirms. He's moved whatever he got out of his bag behind his back. The way he's standing, so military straight, issuing commands, he looks more than ever like Dad.

And, however messed up it may be, my sex only gets wetter.

I obey, both feeling thrilled and disturbed.

He comes up behind me. I can see his reflection in the mirror. He's almost a head taller than me and so much broader. I do look like a child in comparison.

No. Not a child. I just look very petite. *Womanly.* And he's all man.

"That's right," he says, his voice low and husky. "Watch us together in the mirror. Watch how goddamn sexy you are."

Then he reaches down and lifts my dress right up and off over my head. I left my panties behind when I stepped out of them to come over to the counter. The dress had a built-in bra so now I'm completely naked.

Dominick tugs off both his shirts, and then it's just him and me in the mirror.

His hand slides around my waist and down to my soaking sex. His touch is enough to make me insane, but the image of us, naked together in the mirror, his focused gaze intent on where he's touching me—oh God, I shudder and collapse back against him as the spasm rocks through my body.

"Eyes open," he whispers sharply, so I force my eyes open.

He pushes his other finger in my mouth. I suck it even as the waves begin to rocket outward through my body. I watch in confused bliss as he drops his second hand—I think to join the first—but no. Oh—

Oh—!

My eyes shoot open and the orgasm lights even higher as his forefinger nudges and probes at my most forbidden place.

I grab the counter and pitch forward, pinned between it and his body, unable to stop from crying out as the tip of his forefinger penetrates my ass.

I clench around both of his digits as the climax peaks. My whole body goes tight and then expands like a heat bomb explodes from my center.

I barely have a moment to even consider everything that just happened though, because Dominick uses the momentary relaxing of my body to push his finger even further in my back entrance.

I hiss out in shock, my eyes going wide again. My head jerks up as I look at Dominick in the mirror. He was watching for my reaction, I can tell by the way his eyes are narrowed and he's biting his lip in concentration like he does sometimes when we study together.

He planned this.

Maybe not in this exact way, but he always intended to get in my...in my...

He always wanted in *back there*.

My muscles flex and tighten around his finger where it's lodged inside me at the realization.

His pupils dilate even more than they already are and his nostrils flare in reaction.

And an aftershock rocks through my limbs at seeing it.

He is so turned on right now. His scrubs are so thin, I can feel just how hard he is against me. Is he planning to take me there? To stick *it* in there? Right *now*?

Would I let him? Do I want that?

I think of how Dad just shoved in my pussy. I didn't feel ready for that. It hurt *so* bad. Even last night, there was still so much pain involved.

It makes everything so confusing.

With Dominick, at least so far, I've only felt comfort and safety. Not pain. But is he like Dad? He said that he was, earlier. Does he also want to make me cry and taste my tears?

I clench around him again, but this time because part of me wants to pull away. A big part.

"Sarah? What's going on." When I look up again, I see that, though the lust is still there, there's also concern. "What just happened? You can talk to me. If there's anything happening you're not comfortable with, just tell me."

Dominick starts to withdraw his finger but I stop him.

"No," I say quickly. God, this is *Dominick*. As much as they look alike, he's not Dad. "I just..." I bite my lip.

"What? Sarah, I meant it. You can tell me anything." With his hand that was drawing pleasure from my sex just moments ago, he pulls my hair back from my neck and drops a series of sweet, maddening kisses along my shoulder.

I shudder against his lips. "I like everything you do to me. I-I, I'm just not sure I'm ready for you to," I pause again, not wanting to displease him.

"What?"

Again he starts to withdraw his back finger, and again, I clench around him to stop him.

"You can touch me there," I say quickly, "but I just don't think I'm ready to, you know..." my cheeks go pink in the mirror. "...*have sex there*." The last part comes out as a whisper.

Dominick visibly relaxes in the mirror and he smiles.

"I know, babe." He kisses my neck again, sucking and nipping. "That's why I want to prepare you. This is how we do that." And then his finger starts to rotate and move in and out. "I want to show you how good it can feel to have pressure back there while I take you high." His deep voice has my sex clenching and I can't help the little whine that comes out at his words.

"Bend over," he whispers low in my ear. He nips at my ear and then urges me to follow his directions with his hands.

I do and soon I'm lying with my breasts against the cold counter. Ass out. I look in the mirror at Dominick looking down at me in satisfaction.

It's then that I can finally see the small object that he pulls from his pocket where he must have put it earlier. Well, two objects. One of them is a little tube.

The other is a long, thin dildo.

My eyes widen as he squirts gel from the tube on the dildo. Well, is it a dildo if it's not shaped like a penis? It's just long, thin, and looks made of rubber.

The next thing I know, Dominick's clicked something and it starts vibrating.

Immediately I tense up, but Dom's calm, assuring voice has me relaxing again. He puts his hand at the bottom of my spine. "Just relax, hon. It's the same as my fingers. Here, why don't I open you up again first." He looks back down at me.

"Christ," his voice is low, "I love getting my fingers in that sweet, tight little ass of yours. Do you know what a dream come true it will be to take you here, beautiful? Christ, I go crazy just thinking about it."

As he talks, one of his fingers, which he also drenched in gel, starts to probe at my entrance. "Your little body was made for me, do you know that? At the wedding it was fucking killing me to see you dancing with Dad. I wanted to rip his hands off your waist. You were so beautiful. So fucking beautiful."

As he talks, I relax, and his finger slips inside again. He presses the advantage and the tip of another pushes for entry along with the first.

"You're doing so good. Christ, feel how hot and slick you are. Just gobbling up my fingers." His face takes on that look of pained pleasure in the mirror that drives me absolutely insane. And the feeling of what he's doing to me. So foreign. And forbidden.

But it's Dominick.

And the *pressure*.

With how slowly he's going, it doesn't hurt at all. He was right. It does feel *good*. Everything Dominick does feels good. So good. So right.

The second finger slips inside and I jolt in surprise.

Dominick's mouth drops open and he looks just as shocked. And so turned on, I can't even.

"Beautiful, I'm gonna blow in my pants, you're so fucking perfect. Christ— *Christ—*" He stares down at my backside looking absolutely mesmerized, no doubt watching the spot where his fingers disappear into my ass, slowly twisting back and forth and around. Exploring and stretching and—

"I've gotta taste you while I'm in your ass like this," he says suddenly. Then, not removing his fingers, he drops to his knees and swivels so that he's underneath the sink, facing my sex. His forearm is still raised, fingers buried two knuckles deep in my ass.

He lifts up on his knees slightly and then his mouth latches onto my clit.

I was riding a pleasant buzz after my last orgasm while I focused on the sensations of what his fingers were doing to my body, but all the sensations combined together.

So much.

Too much almost.

Oh God, I'm almost immediately at the edge again, except that this time, it's so much higher. I don't know why second orgasms tend to be more explosive than the first, but they are for me. Even more so this time because of the next feelings Dominick has been introducing me to, both physically and emotionally…

The fullness in the back, plus stimulation at the front— Oh my God, I can't—

I clench and clench and bite down on my bottom lip to keep from screaming as the second orgasm rips through me.

Dominick keeps suckling at me and pumping his fingers in and out of my ass through it all. He only stops minutes later when the aftershocks spasming through my legs threaten to make me fall over.

"Can't stand up much longer," I pant. "Too much."

Those too words encapsulate all of it. But God, I still want more. So I tell Dom. "More." My pussy is still aching.

"I need more," I whine, pressing up against Dominick's body when he stands back up and pulls his fingers from my backside. "Another," I say greedily, kissing him hard. "I want another. I need another." I lift a leg around his hips and grind my pussy against his cock.

Pussy.

Cock.

God I love the way those words sound.

"I want you inside me," I growl against his lips.

He nips at my lower lip and groans. "You don't know how much I want that. Christ, and how quickly you come, it's so fucking insane. You're so fucking beautiful." He kisses me hard. "But you're too sore. You need rest down there."

"But you!" I reach down and grab his cock through his scrubs. Ugh, why is he still wearing those. I want to see that gorgeous, beautiful cock of his. I want it now. I shove the waistband of his scrubs down, freeing his glorious dick. It's raging and hard and I *want* it.

I start to drop down to my knees, licking my lips, but Dominick stops me with a firm shake of his head.

"Not today, beautiful. Today is all about you."

"But—" I protest.

"Don't forget," he says, pulling the vibrator back out of his pocket. He's turned it off, but just the sight of the toy makes my breath short. "Your training for the day isn't done yet."

I can't help licking my lips again. Dominick, who's watching my lips, grins.

"Up on the counter." He gestures me to hike myself up on the elevated sink, then lifts me himself when I apparently don't move fast enough for his liking. He hikes my ankles up in the air, relubricates the dildo, and has it nudging at my asshole in moments.

A shudder racks my body at feeling the cold plastic. I look down, and from this angle, I can watch it disappear in my forbidden little hole.

I swallow hard and relax like Dominick instructs. He's right. Because of the stretching he's done, it slides in without any problem at all.

Dominick quickly washes his hands.

And then he turns the dildo on to vibrate again.

Which brings on a whole new slew of sensations. It's far longer than his fingers and he's not hesitant about pushing it in deep. Then deeper. Then deeper still.

Soon I can feel it rumbling so deep inside me. Oh God, I'm so full.

Dominick moves the wand all around and it vibrates up and through my sex. Which is when he naturally begins to play with my pussy again. He leisurely circles my clit, then dips down through my lips, plunges one finger into my channel, then two. Then he starts toying with my clit.

Basically he's freaking torturing me.

Until I grab his arms and jerk him against me, kissing him until both of us are out of breath. With him so close, his cock is caught between our stomachs. Even the feel of it makes my pussy tighten on the fingers he has inside me.

"I want you to come," I say, biting his lower lip. "Come all over me."

He growls and moves back only far enough to grab his shaft. He jerks himself so roughly and I'm fascinated by the sight.

I can't take my eyes off of his hand on his cock. The fluid, masculine movement of him pleasuring himself. It's the most erotic thing I've ever seen in my life.

He's still plunging the dildo in and out of my ass with his other hand. But it's watching him masturbate that has me on the edge again.

"Touch yourself," he orders. "And come when I tell you to. Not a fucking moment before, do you hear me?"

I nod, breathing so hard my chest pumps up and down. I drop a hand down my body. Another forbidden thing. I can't believe I'm about to—

But watching Dominick, the only thing I can think is *God, I need friction.*

It's so insanely hot seeing him like this. The needy strain on his face. The way he grips himself so ruthlessly, dragging the skin up and down, twisting hard around the bulbous head and then just *jerking* back down. Then the way his eyes go slowly unfocused and his mouth is lax with pleasure.

"I said fucking *touch* yourself," he commands. "One hand on your clit, the other buried in your cunt. I want you filthy with your own juices."

I pant as I obey, rushing to circle my clit. I'm so swollen and sensitive down there from coming twice already, my sex jerks as soon as I make contact. I lean back against the mirror and then stick first one finger inside myself and then two. *Oh God*, I've never done that before. Never actually put my fingers inside myself. Ever. I've only touched my clit, and that only tentatively. Always with so much guilt.

My insides feel strange. Hot and soft and stretchy.

Dominick's merciless with the dildo now. He saws it in and out of my ass, but it feels good, so *good*.

"You're so fucking perfect," he says through clenched teeth, his face screwing up with strain and pleasure. "I've never seen anything so goddamned beautiful. Fucking come with me. *Now*."

And I do. I come and I come and I come.

Dominick jerks himself and ropes of cum spray on my stomach and I come so hard I feel like I might black out and my head split in two.

When I can feel my limbs and see again, Dominick is clutching me to him, kissing my face, and he's whispering over and over, "I love you. I love you, Sarah. Christ, I love you so much."

My heart sings even as a loud knock starts up at the door.

I ignore it and grab Dominick's face. "I love you too. Forever." I kiss him hard.

I feel so light, so happy. Maybe it's because we have to scurry to clean up and get our clothes on that Dominick's face becomes shadowed.

Or I'm just imagining it because five minutes later, we're both laughing after the librarian glowered at us, saying there was a noise complaint and asking for our student IDs.

Dominick covered for me saying we'd forgotten them in the dorm and then told me to run for it. He grabbed my hand and we rushed for the stairs.

Yes, as we walk hand in hand toward Dominick's car and I'm more happy and fulfilled than I've ever felt in my life, I'm sure any darkness I glimpsed in Dom's face was just in my imagination.

TEN

That weekend, both Dad and Dominick aren't around at all. After spending Saturday driven crazy by the empty house and a sense of anticipation I can't even fully explain, when I see a note from Dominick saying he's sorry he missed me and that he's working another double, I spend Sunday in the college library working on a big paper that's due Tuesday.

Yes, if Dominick had been around this weekend, I would have totally blown it off, but the semester's almost over and I've been so scatterbrained for months, it's good to focus on school for a little while. Burying myself in research about Piaget's stages of cognitive development is *almost* enough to keep my mind off everything at home.

We've managed family dinners twice since Dominick's and my interlude in the library bathroom and everything has been, well...wonderful.

Dad smiles at the secret looks Dominick and I shoot each other. Both of them squeeze my butt playfully when I pass on the way to set the table or while we're doing the dishes or heading to the den to watch after dinner TV. But that's as far as it's gone. Everything's settled back into our normal routine—with just an edge of playfulness to it.

Dad helped me with my Statistics homework on Thursday and afterward stopped me with a hand on my arm. "I know the adjustment of Dominick and I coming to live with you must have taken some getting used to." His voice softened. "Especially as we get even closer as a family and our relationships become complex." He reached out and took my hand, his thumb my caressing my inner wrist.

"But I want you to know that getting to know you has been one of the best things that's ever happened to us. It's brought Dominick and I closer than ever before as well. You're such a special young woman." With that he gave my hand one last squeeze, leaned over and kissed my forehead. Then he got up and left the kitchen.

I stayed there at the table, feeling warm all the way through. Then it was followed by anxiety as I looked after him. What did all that mean? Would he want to come to my room tonight? Was I ready for that? But no, Dominick said it was only something they'd do together from now on. That calmed me down.

And true to what Dominick had said, Dad didn't come that night. Was it just because Dominick wasn't home? And did that mean that the first night both of them *were* there, they'd want to…? After all, Dominick had the vibrator because he said he wanted to train and prepare me for…

But both of them haven't been home at the same time. Dominick's still working crazy hours. Even Dad's been gone more than usual as the hospital scrambles to get in as many donor dollars as possible by the board's deadline if the new oncology wing of the hospital is to be a go. I know he's stressed out by it all even though he tries to leave work behind at work.

I try hard not to let any of my own stress show. Yes, I have classes, but it's also the lingering uncertainty about things here at home.

I'd hate for either Dad or Dominick to guess that they're the cause of any anxiety. And the further I get from that initial sexual experience, the more convinced I am that I was just immature in my response to it all. Of course sex hurt the first time—I was a virgin for God's sake. My hymen had to break. Um hello? Facts of biology much?

Plus, even though I haven't seen as much as I'd like of Dominick —well, to be honest, I've barely seen him at all—he's been leaving little treats for me in my bureau where I keep my hair and makeup things.

God, I blush even thinking about it. The first time I opened the drawer to pull out my brush and saw what he'd left me, I yelped and almost slammed it shut again. Like I was embarrassed someone else might see or something. Ridiculous, since obviously there was no one else there. I was still absurdly embarrassed about reopening the drawer and reading the note in Dominick's messy doctor's handwriting.

Wear this whenever you can over the next couple days. Leave it in while you go to school and think of me. Prepare yourself for me, beautiful.

Beside the note was a small anal plug and a small tube of lubricant.

Every few days, he'd leave a larger plug and a new note.

You can't imagine what it does to me, imagining you walking around with my present inside you. I'm so hard all the time I can barely concentrate. Soon, beautiful, you'll be mine in every way.

And after another few days, after the long weekend spent tucked away at the library on my paper, I finally see him. It's Tuesday morning. I stayed up most of last night finishing the paper and barely had time to shower, then dash downstairs and grab a croissant before running out the door. He's just coming in, looking exhausted after a night shift.

"Beautiful," he says in happy surprise when he opens the door to find me on the other side, just slinging my backpack and purse over my shoulder.

"Dominick!" I immediately drop my backpack and fling my arms around him. "I've missed you so much." I kiss him and he pulls me up and into his body, kissing me back just as ferociously.

"Don't forget to breathe, you two," Dad says, walking over to the both of us.

Dad turns me to him and kisses me on the lips as well. Dominick's lips were warm and tasted like chocolate. Which makes me smile because I know it's one of his tricks when he's tired at work —he sneaks little dark chocolates to help himself stay awake.

Dad's lips are cool and minty. He's probably just drank some of the bracingly cold filtered water from the fridge. And brushed his teeth.

As soon as Dad pulls back, my eyes shoot over to Dominick. Will he be mad that Dad kissed me?

No, he's still just smiling at me like he's never been happier to see anyone in his life. Relief sweeps over me.

I lean up on my tiptoes and kiss Dom again.

Mmm. Chocolate. His tongue tangles with mine, and then there's a warm body at my back and hands cupping my ass.

Dad squeezes and kneads my backside through my jeans, then grinds himself into me, pressing me into Dominick.

"Sweet, sweet girl," Dad whispers. "Look at you so hot for your big brother." His breath is warm on the back of my neck since my hair is up in a ponytail.

"But you can't be late to school," he continues and pulls away, but not without a solid *wallop* to my backside.

I yelp but then giggle.

Dominick withdraws from my mouth, though not without holding me for another long second before releasing me.

"You need a ride to school?" he asks, searching my eyes.

I smile at his sweetness. He's just come off a God-knows-how-long shift and he's offering to drive me to school?

"I'm fine. Get some sleep."

"I'll take her," Dad says. "She's on my way."

"I can just take the bus like I usually do," I start to protest, but both men are already shaking their head.

"It looks like rain," Dominick says, then he looks over to Dad. "You got her?"

Dad rubs my shoulder and drops another kiss there. "Always."

A look I can decipher passes between the two men, then Dad picks up my backpack from the ground. "Let's get going, sweet girl. Don't want to be late."

I reach out and squeeze Dom's hand, then I'm out the door with Dad.

Dominick was right, it does start to rain on the way to my school and I'm glad not to be out in it. It only takes about twenty minutes to get there and for a while Dad and I just listen to NPR morning news.

When we're about five minutes away, Dad turns off the radio. I look over at him in surprise.

He watches the road, the windshield wipers flipping furiously to clear the rain from the window.

"I'm really looking forward to the Father-Daughter Dance on Thursday."

"Me too." I smile over at him and his eyes flick off the road for a second toward me.

"Do you have a dress ready?"

I nod, then realize his eyes are back on the road. "Yep. Grandpa gave me a wardrobe allowance just for this sort of thing. I got a really nice one this weekend."

"What color is it?" Dad's question comes out sharp and for some reason, I feel like this is some sort of test.

"Mauve," I say, not knowing what the right answer is. I clarify more, "Sort of a soft pink."

Dad relaxes and smiles. "Good." He takes another quick glance at me. "Just needed to know what color corsage I should get."

"Oh," I respond, still a little confused.

Then he reaches a hand out and puts it on my knee. "I'm so

proud of you that you know how to dress like a young lady. Not be like so many other girls your age and dress like a slut."

He pulls to the side of the road in front of my English building and leans over. "Except when you're being Daddy's little slut, of course." He nips my earlobe with his teeth and I can't help the intake of breath his words evoke.

I blink when he pulls back.

He makes everything sound so dirty.

But I'm squirming in my jeans at the same time.

Dad's certainly a lot more crass than Dominick. But I think that's just his way. He likes to get this response out of me.

The fact that I currently have the third size up anal plug in my backside right now isn't helping matters. The truth is, both of them are dirty as hell, and they're both drawing me into their games in their own way.

Dad's hand on my knee moves so that he's rubbing up and down my thigh, creeping further and further inward. "Have a wonderful day, sweet girl," he says in a low voice, those green eyes of his burning with intensity. Like he's daring me to stay in the car with him.

"Okay, bye!" I say and then jerk the car door open. I sprint through the rain the short distance to the building and use my body to push open the door.

By the time I look back through the glass door, breathing so hard I'm panting like I've just run a mile, Dad's car is gone.

ELEVEN

Thursday comes around far too quickly. I feel like the Father-Daughter Dance carries a symbolic significance. Like Dad and I going out into the world officially as father and daughter makes it, I don't know, more real.

He's introducing me to the world of his colleagues and friends as his daughter.

Yes, that sort of happened at the wedding, but I barely knew him then. I certainly didn't call him Dad back then and our level of intimacy was nothing to what it is now.

I spend over two hours getting ready, between the shower and primping and hair and makeup. At first I try for a fancy, mature updo, but at the last minute instinctively know that Dad won't like it. My makeup is too heavy, too. The dark eye makeup I opted for gives me an air of sophistication that *I* like—but I can just see him frowning at it. So the last half hour is spent using my makeup remover cream and rushing as I start all over.

I go for natural and simplistic. Instead of lipstick, I opt for a shiny lip-gloss that has the slightest pink tint. My hair still has some curl to it from the attempted updo, but now it hangs in long dark waves down my back, pinned simply at the sides to frame my face.

It all makes me look very young.

I bet Dad will love it.

I step into the dress and carefully zip it up as high as I can reach. Then I head over to Dominick's room, where I knock on his door.

He opens it, looking absolutely gorgeous in a tux. His eyes immediately widen when he takes me in.

"Holy shit, Sarah," he breathes out. "You're a goddess."

I laugh at his overreaction and turn around, lifting my hair to the side. "Zip me up?"

Even though it's officially a Father-Daughter Dance, other members of family and plus-ones are welcome at the event.

Dominick's fingers caress the skin of my back, tracing up my spine and making me shiver before he follows it by zipping up my dress.

I turn back around, smoothing down the skirt of the dress. It's a sleeveless silk chiffon floor-length gown with a sweetheart neckline, tailored to fit my petite frame perfectly. I've got on a pair of silver strappy pumps that give me a few extra inches so that I almost reach Dominick's chin.

"Are you sure I look okay?" I ask nervously.

"You look gorgeous." He leans down to kiss me but I smack him away.

"Don't! You'll mess up my makeup. I want Dad to see me while everything still looks perfect."

He grins down at me. "My little perfectionist." He holds out his arm. "Shall we?"

I can't help the little melty-swoon thing my heart does. God, he really is heart-stoppingly handsome. "You don't look so bad yourself," I manage through my suddenly dry throat. Then I take his arm and he leads me down the stairs.

Dad's reaction is similarly gratifying. He's waiting for us at the bottom of the stairs.

"Sweet girl, you've never been more beautiful. I could eat you up." He takes me from Dominick's arm, and before I can say anything about mussing my makeup, he's devouring my mouth. Well, at least I brought my gloss to refresh in the little clutch I grabbed at the last minute.

"Come on, Dad," Dominick quips. "Don't want to be late to your big event. All the donors will be there, after all."

Dad comes up for air and claps Dom on the back. For a second, there's the slightest bit of tension that I sometimes think I sense between the two of them, but the next second, Dad's laughing and ushering me out the door.

To a limo that's waiting on the curb.

A *limo*.

I look back at Dad and shake my head.

He's grinning at me, obviously watching and waiting to see my reaction. "What did you do?" I ask.

"Like Dominick said," Dad's grin widens. "It's my party. Got to arrive in style." As he walks forward, the driver steps out and comes around to open the door for us. Dad raises a hand and gestures for me to get in first. "My lady," he says, bowing.

I laugh at how ridiculous he's being and take his hand as he helps me into the car. Dominick is there too, lifting my dress so I don't accidently step on it while I get in. It feels like a fairytale. Except that Cinderella was never lucky enough to have *two* Prince Charmings.

I sit down, still feeling overwhelmed. And we aren't even at the party yet.

A COUPLE HOURS later and the sense of being dazed hasn't abated.

The ball is held in a high-rise hotel downtown and it's clear no expense was spared. The crystal chandeliers are part of the hotel, but each table drips with huge, exotic flower arrangements. The tableware is all exquisite, the band fantastic.

I've lost count of the times Dad has introduced me as, "my beautiful daughter." He's recounted the story of his lonely existence before marrying my mother and how he never expected to inherit the amazing gift of a ready-made family.

You'd never know Mom's not part of the picture with the happy-family portrait he paints. But really, apart from her fictional presence, I have to admit that everything he says feels completely true.

I was so achingly lonely before they moved in. And now everything is rich and full because of them. I have family now. The fact that I get an entire glamorous evening out with them just seems like icing on the cake.

And seriously—the cake is crazy delicious. The entire meal is gourmet. Seared salmon with asparagus, peppers and baby potatoes. Then the most amazing and gorgeous little individual chocolate cakes.

Dominick could see how absolutely enthralled I was by mine and he gave me his. I know, Dominick, he of the hollow leg, actually sacrificing a scrumptious dessert? If that doesn't say love, I don't know what does. But by now, I know that that's just who he is—always taking care of me in every way he can.

And if I didn't already suspect that tonight was *the* night, he confirmed when he texted me that when I went to the bathroom, I should also stretch out my pussy with several fingers so that I'd be completely comfortable later.

I'd never even considered that, but what a good idea. Pre-stretching. Just like for the gym. But for, you know, other very athletic *activities*. I snickered to myself even as I secreted away to the bathroom, lifted my beautiful, dainty pink dress, and fingered myself. Such a dirty and delicious little secret.

I washed my hands twice afterwards, but swore I could still smell myself when I sipped at my sparkling cider while Dad was up at the podium making a speech about how the expansion of the oncology ward would never have been possible without the gracious donors present tonight.

They just found out yesterday right before he came home the hospital met their fundraising goal. Tonight really is a celebration in every meaning of the word.

"And now," Dad announces from the podium, "Let the dancing begin. I invite all fathers and daughters to the dance floor. I myself am so excited to welcome my newest addition to the family—my lovely daughter Sarah—to dance with me tonight." He holds out a hand in the direction of our table. "Sarah?"

Heads swing in my direction and I feel my stupid cheeks heat. But I hate the idea of disappointing Dad, so I hurry to my feet.

Please don't trip. Oh God, please don't let me trip.

Squaring my shoulders, I smile as brightly as possible and walk toward Dad where he's moved to the center of the dance floor.

Dad beams at me, white teeth on display, green eyes flashing brilliantly under the chandelier. He looks more handsome than ever.

When he raises one arm and rests his other hand at my waist, I'm so glad that I'm not the ignorant little girl I was all those months ago who didn't even know how to dance. If life is all about discovering who you are, then the last six months have been one helluva crash course.

I grin at the thought as I confidently lift one hand to his and put the other on his shoulder. The music starts and he begins rocking me back and forth as a sweet, sentimental song plays through the speakers.

The dance floor fills up with other father-daughter couples and we're soon lost in the crowd. Dad pulls me tighter against him and as the song progresses, I lay my head against his chest.

I feel the déjà vu of the first time we danced like this. When this man entered my life and I got just an inkling of how important he was going to be to me. I hadn't even realized about Dominick yet. I had no clue just how deep the intimacies would go. Maybe I still don't.

Tonight.

I squirm against the fullness in my backside. Part of me thought there was no way I should keep the plug in for such a fancy occasion as tonight.

But a little devil inside wondered—how deliciously naughty would it be to be dressed up so innocently in this perfect pink dress, all the while having a toy buried inside my *ass*, reminding me of exactly what Dominick wants to do to me later? The devil won.

Imagining Dominick's constant state of arousal has kept me in a state of near permanent stimulation all week. I haven't done anything about it either. That felt like cheating. And knowing that tonight is coming…whatever tonight might be…

God, the only thing that kept me from coming when I was stretching my pussy earlier in the women's restroom was the steady stream of traffic in and out of the other bathroom stalls. I didn't think I could stifle my cries if I'd let myself even begin to go there.

Plus, I've waited this long. What's a few more hours?

"You're such a good girl," Dad whispers in my ear. "You've waited so patiently."

Whoa. I look up at him sharply. It's like he can read my thoughts. Did Dominick tell him about the plugs?

"I've been patient too," he continues. "Dominick said we needed to let you heal fully." His grip on my hand tightens as his voice lowers. "But sweet girl, Daddy's missed you."

When I look back into his eyes, they're filled with such raw need and desire, he looks like he's about to throw me onto the ground in the middle of all these people and have at me right here.

But then as if he too realizes just where we are, he pulls back from me and softens his features into something more benign. "Good things come to those who wait." It's a mutter, and I can't tell if he's reminding me or himself.

The song continues to play, and right as the last notes ring out, there are hands suddenly jerking me backwards out of Dad's grip.

What the—?

"So this is my replacement?"

A woman wearing a tight black dress with her hair in pigtails has a grip on my forearm so tight she's going to leave claw-marks from her sharp nails.

"Ow, let me go!" I jerk away from her but she's got a death grip. She shakes me roughly, still glaring at Dad.

"What does she have that I don't?" she shrieks.

Now that I get a better look at her, I see that she's got carefully applied makeup to try to make herself look doll-like. Rosy cheeks, eye makeup intended to make her eyes look larger, lipstick painted in a little rosebud mouth even though it's not her mouth's natural shape.

While from far away I bet the effect is impressive, from close up, it's just grotesque.

Dad advances on her, his features twisted in disgust. "Get out of here, Janine. I told you I don't want you anymore."

Her nails pinch into my skin even harder. "You don't mean that!"

Dad glares at her, standing taller and towering over the both of us. "You're causing a scene," he hisses underneath his breath. He's not wrong. Heads all around us have turned to see what's going on.

"I don't care," Janine says. "They need to know. *I'm* your little girl. Not *her*."

She still has hold of me me but her words are such a blow, I stagger back and she finally loses her grip. She's too busy trying to get close to Dad.

I blink.

"Sarah, are you okay?" Dominick runs up and catches me before I stumble into anyone in the crowd that's circling around us.

Janine whips around at his voice. "Dommie, make Daddy listen to me!" she cries.

Her words are like an arrow piercing my heart.

She starts to come at Dominick now but Dad catches her in his arms and starts to lead her away through the crowd. She clutches onto his lapels but looks over her shoulder at where Dominick holds onto me. "No, I want Dommie too. It's not right without the both of you!"

I double over, feeling all the breath knocked out of me. Dominick rubs my back but I pull away from him.

Air. I need air. I start to move as quickly as my stupid heels will let me in the opposite direction Dad took *that woman*.

No, he's not your Dad.

God, how pathetic have I been all this time?

What number am I anyway?

How many times have they done this?

How many women?

And I felt so special.

I thought all this happened spontaneously.

So naturally.

Because we were family. I thought that word *meant* something.

God, I'm so *stupid*.

I get to the edge of the dance floor and yank off my shoes, hike up my gown and start to run.

"Sarah," Dominick calls. "Wait. Sarah!"

I keep running, up some stairs to the area that leads to the hotel lobby. But even with my shoes off, of course my strides are nothing to Dominick's long legs. He catches up to me easily and grabs me around the waist.

"No." I hit at his chest as he tries to hold me. "Let go of me. I don't want to hear your excuses!"

"Stop. Wait, it's not what you—"

I smack at his chest, his shoulders, his face. He ducks out of the way and tries again. "Sarah, just give me a second—"

But I don't want to. No seconds will be given. I'm done being made a fool of. Stupid naïve little Sarah, is that what they thought? And God, I was, wasn't I?

I just keep hitting his chest, so furious. It hurts, God, I never thought anything could hurt this bad, and I want to make him hurt—

"Stop it," Dominick says again, and this time he grabs both of my wrists in a single one of his hands. I wrestle against his hold but it's no use. Stupid boys being so strong. I growl in frustration as I continue trying to free my hands.

His cheeks are spotted pink with frustration as he glares down at me. "If you're going to act like a little girl, so help me I'll flip you over my shoulder like one and take you somewhere I'll make you listen," he threatens.

I scoff at him and roll my eyes.

And the next thing I know I'm ass over head as he flips me up and over his shoulder.

"Let me down!" I shriek. "You giant— Oaf!" I finish for lack of a better insult.

He pushes open a door and when I look around, still disoriented from, you know—being upside down!—I realize we're in yet another bathroom stall.

"Oh no you don't, mister," I growl. "You better not even think I'm going to—"

But suddenly the world is being flipped topsy turvy again as he sets me back on my feet. Apparently the multi-stall bathroom is empty, because Dominick locks the door. Then he stands in front of it and crosses his arms over his chest like some kind of Viking sentry.

"What are you— You can't just—" I try to pull him out of the way and get to the door but he's a giant and completely immovable.

I let out a huge huff of frustration and cross my own arms over my chest. I turn my back to him. Which doesn't really help because I can still see his reflection in the multiple bathroom mirrors. Stubbornly, I squeeze my eyes shut.

"You can lock me in here until someone notifies hotel security, but I'm not going to talk to you." I jut my chin out.

"Fine," he says, breathing out so loudly I can hear how frustrated he is. Even without looking I can imagine the hand he's running through his floppy locks.

Dammit, I hate that I know him so well.

No, Sarah, that's not true. You don't know him at all. It was just a trick. Pretend intimacy. Really this has just been a whole big scam. A game he and his dad have played many, many times before. The thought is a spear through the chest and I want to go curl up in a stall and put a barrier between us, even if it's as feeble as a bathroom stall door.

"You won't talk, then listen. Janine is not a healthy woman. We didn't know that when we started dating her. And yes, we *both* dated her at the same time. It was something we tried for a while."

I wince and take a step away from him. In spite of my determination not to say anything, I have to ask the question. "How many women? Have you shared?"

Another loud expulsion of breath from him. And then silence.

Oh my God. There have been so many he can't even remember—

"Five."

I blink. Was that more or fewer than I was expecting?

More than I wanted.

Fewer than my horrible imaginings had started cooking up.

I rub my hands up and down my arms. "How did it start?"

I turn around to look at him.

He's dropped his arms but hasn't moved from the door. His eyes are pleading. For me to understand? Not to leave them?

"It started with my high school tutor."

I jerk back from him. What? I didn't expect that. "How old were you?"

His eyes are clear and steady as he answers. "Seventeen."

My mouth drops open. "She abused you."

He shrugs. "I didn't really think of it like that at the time. She was only twenty-one. I was getting laid so I was happy. I was combining my Junior and Senior year so I felt old enough. She was hot."

"Dominick, that doesn't make it okay—"

"Yeah well, that's not all. Turns out she was sleeping with Dad too."

My mouth which I'd just closed drops wide open again. "What a bitch!"

Dominick laughs at my reaction. "Dad caught us together, but it was after I'd just turned eighteen. For all he knew, she hadn't come onto me until I was of age. Anyway, she got super freaked out that he was going to get pissed and fly off the handle."

Dominick shrugs again. "He didn't. He just came and joined in. Well, Dad being Dad," he rolls his eyes, "she got her punishment, but in Dad's way."

"And you were..." I pause, not knowing how to put this delicately, "*okay* with that?"

He looks down. "Dad and I have always had a... how do I put this... a complex relationship. I was mad at the woman for cheating on me with Dad. I mean, him busting us like that was how I found out about it. I was hurt—she'd been my first and I guess, I don't know." He looks up at me and smiles self-deprecatingly.

"I thought our feelings for each other went deeper than they obviously did. I guess I thought both of us doing her like that would be fucking her over somehow." He shakes his head. "Turned out she was really into it. We kept it up all three of us for a little while but it fizzled. Dad got a new girlfriend and I guess I was still upset about the tutor, so I..." he trails off and his dark eyes come back up to me. "I'm not proud of this part." He pauses like he doesn't want to go on.

Hesitantly, I take a step forward. "Tell me. I want to know." I swallow. "All of it."

He looks down. "Well, I knew he had this new girlfriend, so I seduced her." He glances up, eyes wary and obviously bracing for my reaction. "To get back at him. I told you I was really competitive with him for a while. So that's what we did. We'd sort of compete with women, sleeping with women together but secretly each trying to one-up the other."

I stumble back again. "Is that what you're trying to do with me?" I think of how each of them have come to me separately, with their different seductive styles, and my stomach starts to churn.

"God, no!" Dominick says, finally moving away from the door and coming toward me.

I hold up a hand to keep him back, though. He seems so sincere, but can I really trust him after all he's just admitted to me?

"Tell me about Janine."

He swallows hard but doesn't look away. I can already tell I'm not going to like what I'm about to hear.

"I was getting older, I'd started my residency at the hospital and Dad and I were trying to bury the hatchet. Change things between us. I wanted to just start dating women on my own, but Dad convinced me to keep doing what we were doing, but go about in a different way. We decided we'd go into a relationship with everyone knowing ahead of time what they were getting into. Dad obviously has certain kinks he likes to play out." He looks at me knowingly and I nod, getting what he means. The whole Daddy thing. "So we went looking for a woman who liked to play the same way. We found Janine at a BDSM club Dad had heard about."

My eyes obviously must've widened at the acronym because Dominick raises both his hands. "Neither of us are into the rest of that stuff, but it's not exactly like you can put out an ad on Craiglist and say, looking for a girl who likes you to spank her and call you Daddy." He winces. "Well, I'm sure you could, but," he cringes. "…enough said."

"Anyway, we thought we might find someone with similar, you know, appetites. But it was just a disaster. Janine was fun at first, but she was really needy. It was clear almost from the start. And soon it was bordering on stalking."

"Whoa."

"Yeah." He nods. "She'd show up at our jobs, dressed up in these bizarre little girl outfits, crying and making scenes when Dad or I wouldn't see her. We had to get restraining orders. It turns out she's bipolar and has a coke habit on top of it. We paid for her to go to rehab once, but we'd only dated her for a month," he lifts his hands, "and there was only so much we felt we could do for her that wasn't just encouraging her obsession. We talked to the club where we met her and one of her old Doms said he'd talk to her family and see if they could help. The last time we'd heard from her was when we had to call the police on her a month before Dad married your mom."

Which he'd done because he needed Grandpa's influence and connections. I saw plenty of Grandpa's friends around the ballroom tonight. Donors for the new wing when Dad had needed the last influx of new money to shore up the project. Because of Grandpa, I guessed, it was made possible. His old money friends had deep pockets.

"And then you met me?" I question, putting the last piece of the puzzle in place.

Dominick nods. "And you were like no one and nothing I'd ever seen before."

I stand there, processing everything he's said.

"Please, can I hold you now?" He steps forward before stopping again, eyebrows scrunched together as if pained. "You're killing me here."

God, does he think he's the only one? Doubting him, wondering if everything I thought I knew was a lie? I've been dying inside ever since that woman put her hands on me in the ballroom.

But if everything Dominick's said is true, then it's just that—the past. It's naïve to imagine that they would come to me with a completely blank slate. Dominick is twenty-four. And Dad obviously twenty years older than that. They didn't know me. It's not fair to judge them on the things they did then.

"We never imagined we'd ever find someone as perfect as you," Dominick whispers, taking another step forward. "You have no idea. I'd given up even hoping for it. But then I met you. And like I said, that first night at the wedding, your beauty, your innocence, God, you just stood out like this bright beacon apart from everyone else at that party."

I swallow hard as he finally crosses the last bit of space between us. He doesn't crowd me or try to kiss me. He just reaches down and takes both of my hands. His touch is tentative.

I crack the second I feel his warm skin touch mine. I fling myself into his arms.

"Oh God, Dom," I breathe out, squeezing his waist. "I was so scared it was all a lie."

His arms come around me and hold me to him just as fiercely. "Never. Christ, Sarah. Never doubt what I feel for you. I love you. I swear I've never said those words to another woman and I never will. You're my first and my last."

I shake my head against his chest. "It just all seems too good to be true."

He clutches me tighter.

His chest buzzes against my cheek. He must have his cell in his coat pocket. He ignores it but it keeps buzzing away, the person obviously calling back a second time.

"Do you need to get that?" I finally ask.

He sighs. "I'm sure it's just Dad wondering where we are."

"Oh," I pull back. "You should let him know."

Dominick looks down at me and I can't quite read the expression on his face. "Is that what you want?"

I nod, not sure what he expects my answer to be. "Well... yeah? I want him to know I'm okay. After what happened."

Dominick takes the phone out of his pocket but still his finger pauses before pushing the button to call back. The phone starts to vibrate again. He puts a hand underneath my chin, making sure I'm looking him straight in the eye. "If I answer this, Dad will have certain expectations about tonight and what happens next. Are you ready for that?"

He holds up the buzzing phone. "You don't have to do anything you don't want to do. I can turn off my phone and I can take you anywhere you want to go if you feel like today has been too much already. We could go catch a movie or grab a hotdog from a street vendor and walk the streets for hours." His eyes search mine back and forth, his face dead earnest. "Whatever you want. It's always your decision. Your call."

I can tell he means it, absolutely. And his words, combined with knowing that he'll be by my side every step of the way, gives me the courage to take the phone from him, touch the answer button, and answer, "Daddy? Come and get us."

TWELVE

Dad takes over the scene immediately as we get in the hotel room upstairs.

"Dominick, take your sister's dress off. Then baby," he addresses me, eyes dark as he snaps his fingers, pointing at the floor, "on your hands and knees."

My stomach does a flip-flop of anxiety at the command in Dad's voice, but I can't deny the corresponding trickle of wetness in my sex.

Dominick obeys, unzipping my dress and helping me step out of it. Again I relied on the dress's built in bra, so I'm bare up top, with just a scrap of lacy white underwear on. Dominick helps me as I get down to my knees. My legs are so wobbly, I'm grateful for his strong hand holding mine. My eyes ping back and forth between Dominick's confident, caring smile and Dad's dark, brooding features.

Dad's jaw ticks as he pulls his bowtie off and he throws it to the floor. He's had the same look of strain on his features ever since he came and found us outside the lobby men's room.

"You were a very naughty girl, running away like that without letting us explain," Dad says, his eyes darkening even further. He takes off his suitcoat and undoes the buttons of his dress shirt, looking colder and more furious every second.

Alarmed, I look back at Dominick. He's watching Dad, but he reaches down and gives my shoulder a squeeze. My breath evens out at his calm look. While last time we were all together like this, he seemed to take a subordinate role to Dad, this time, he's standing right beside me. He too starts to undress, but at a leisurely pace.

"She was a naughty girl," Dominick agrees. "I think we'll enjoy giving our little girl her punishment, don't you think?"

My eyes shoot up to Dom, but he just shoots me a wink. He's got his shirt off now and damn, he looks so mouth-watering standing over me in just his dress-trousers, his gloriously broad chest on display, unruly hair swept to the side. He's more built even than Dad, his arm muscles bulging. He's toed off his shoes and pulled off his socks, and I swear, even his feet are manly. Him standing over me, so godlike and glorious is such a turn on. As if he can read my thoughts, he grins deviously.

"Look at our sweet little girl's tight ass, just waiting for us," Dominick says. He reaches down and grabs my ass cheeks roughly, massaging and separating them.

It's then that he pauses and looks at me in surprise.

I guess he didn't expect me to have the plug in tonight.

A brief look of alarm crosses his face but then he smiles in a way that seems a little fake as he looks up at Dad. "Little sister is ready for us. I've been preparing her."

"What do you mean?" Dad's voice, already on edge, gets slightly darker.

"I wanted tonight to be perfect for her," Dominick says, all confidence. Then he grabs my underwear at the back, right above my ass and rips them down the middle. The next second, he's tugging the butt plug out and tossing it to the side.

"God you don't know how I've dreamed about this, beautiful." He crouches down and *oh*—

His tongue is—

There.

He's licking at my back entrance around and around. I'm already sensitive from the plug being in there all day and—

"What the hell are you doing?" Dad's angry voice jolts me out of the pleasure induced haze I started drifting into.

Especially when he shoves Dominick away from me, knocking him to the ground. The floor is carpeted, but still, Dom barely catches himself from landing face first.

And Dad's not nearly done.

He grabs my arm and drags me up off the floor, yanking me behind him. "You've been corrupting your sister? Turning my sweet girl into a whore?" Dad's face is red as he starts to unbuckle the shiny black belt from around his waist. I thought it was a strange addition to his tux, but I should have known he wore it for just this purpose. I shrink back at the fury on his face as he advances on Dominick.

"Assume the position," Dad orders.

But Dominick jumps to his feet, fists clenched. "No."

Dad looks shocked for a moment and then his face gets even redder. "What did you say to me?"

Dominick's jaw locks. "I said no. We do this together as equals or not at all. Sarah is still as sweet and pure as ever." He sidesteps Dad and walks over to me. "She's precious and beautiful and perfect just as she is. Nothing could change that."

Dominick puts his hand around my waist and I swallow hard, both at his words and at the horrible tension in the room.

The way he's standing up to Dad. For both himself and for me—God, I want to both cry and hug him and—

Then Dominick's hand around my waist drops down and smacks my ass.

Not hard—but *still!*

I look up at him, open mouthed.

He's grinning down at me. "Now, I'm still all for punishing the little brat," he says. "But only when it's accompanied by pleasure."

His other hand drops down the front of my body and starts to play with my clit.

Then he looks back at Dad, eyes only going slightly hard. "I'm gonna take baby sister's tight ass tonight. I think it would make her feel amazing to have another cock filling up her sweet little cunt at the same time."

He smacks my ass again with another loud *crack*. I yelp even though it barely hurt. When I glance up at Dad, his teeth are gritted together. But he also seems confused, like he's not sure what to think about this turn of events.

Dominick doesn't wait for him to figure it out. He just leads me over to the bed and bends me over it, ass out.

"Are you going to give her the rest of her punishment, or should I?" Dominick asks. I turn my face to the side on the mattress and look back at Dad.

Dad glares at Dominick for a second. "Don't think I'm going to forget this."

I twist to look over my shoulder at where Dominick stands behind me, but he doesn't look intimidated or worried in the least. "In or out, old man?"

Dad immediately springs into action at that. He doesn't charge Dominick again, though. Nope, he comes straight for me.

I'm expecting it, but I still cry out when his palm lands hard on the round of my ass. "Daddy's going to fuck you so hard tonight," he growls, almost immediately landing another blow. "The two of you conspiring behind my back." And then another, right below where he spanked me the first time. "A man does all he can for his children and this is how he's repaid?"

After spanking me several more times he flips me over like I'm nothing more than a rag doll.

And it probably means I'm more than screwed up, but being handled so roughly... God it's turning me *on*.

Dominick joins us on the bed as Dad crawls up and over me. I know nothing will get out of hand with him here. And the charged electricity between all of us makes the pulse between my legs more intense than I've ever felt it before.

"You're gonna swallow Daddy's cock like a good little girl now," Dad says, grabbing me and pulling me onto his lap where he proceeds to shove his giant dick in my mouth. I'm not quite ready and I cough and sputter around it.

"Aw fuck, that's right, little girl. Fucking choke on it." He shoves himself in and out of my mouth and against the inside of my cheek. When he misses my mouth, he slaps the fat head of his cock against my cheek.

"Suck it. Suck it." Then he grabs the hair at the back of my head and shoves me back on his cock.

At the same time, Dominick has dropped low and pried my legs apart. With his tongue and fingers, he toys with my pussy.

I groan around Daddy's dick and struggle to lick and suck on him while he shoves himself roughly in and out of my mouth.

Dominick latches on my clitoris right as Daddy shoves himself so deep he starts to go down my throat.

I struggle and gag around him but he grabs the back of my head and forces himself in a little deeper. Dominick sucks even harder and —*can't breathe*—

Panic and pleasure fight against one another until Daddy finally pulls me off him. I gasp for breath just long enough to get a huge lungful right before he jams himself back in deep again.

It's disorienting, being so out of control of my own body. If it were just me and Daddy, I'd be terrified and freaking out, but Dominick is here. I trust him completely. He thinks this will bring me pleasure.

I'm not supposed to be in control.

So I give myself up to it.

To them.

I mean, I can't help still gagging—it's my body's natural instinct to try to get air when Daddy's choking me with his ungodly large cock. But I try to relax my throat as much as possible. I try to suck him when I can. I want to be a good girl for them.

And when Dominick's talented tongue and fingers stretching me do their work and I can't stand it anymore, I scream a choked howl around Daddy's cock.

Daddy yanks me off him moments later, his eyes dark with a look I've come to recognize. It's a mixture of hunger and lust.

"That's right," he growls, "cry for Daddy, sweet girl." He rubs his palm downward from my eye, smearing the little bit of mascara I'm wearing down my cheeks. I can tell because when he pulls his hand away, they come away with black on them.

"I have to fuck my innocent little baby now. Look how hard you've made Daddy's cock. Look at it." He grabs the hair at the back of my head again and jerks me so that I look down at the huge cock he was just choking me.

Holy crap, it looks even bigger than last time. I wasn't even taking a third of him into my mouth, no matter how far he was trying to jam himself down my throat.

"Get underneath her, Dad," Dominick orders. "Near the edge of the bed."

Dad glares at Dominick, but when his hungry look comes back to me, he complies. He smiles, a slightly manic glint entering his eyes that I've seen before. "Time to cry again for Daddy."

I blink even as he moves himself to the edge of the bed and drops to his back. Then he drags me down and lifts me by my waist to straddle him.

I think I've just realized something.

I think that deep down, some part of Dad actually really *wants* to... *hurt me*.

That it's part of what gets him off.

Does Dominick know?

I don't even have time to consider the question before Dad's grasping my hips, lining himself up, and then pistoning his cock up and into me.

It's shocking, of course. He's so huge and long.

But unlike the past two times, it doesn't feel like he's splitting me in two.

Between stretching myself earlier in the bathroom and Dominick doing the same while he was suckling me just a moment ago, when my breath hitches at Dad's continuing penetration, it's only with pleasure.

Especially when I feel Dominick's warmth at my back.

He's here. He hasn't left me.

"Fuck baby," Dad says, ramming himself in and out like he's making an Olympic sport out of screwing me. "You're so tight. Fucking just-virgin pussy is fucking heaven." His eyes drop closed and his face screws tight with bliss.

Dominick's finger, slick with lube, presses at my asshole as he sweeps my hair to the side and kisses the nape of my neck. "You still want this, beautiful girl?"

He teases the rim of my back entrance, Dad still pumping away inside me, his hands clutching my hips for dear life.

I look over my shoulder at Dominick. I can already feel how flushed I am. God. It's ridiculous. Dad is fucking my brains out, my body jolting every other second with his cock bottoming out, but I still feel a little shy almost about Dominick doing...*that*. It's been so built up—what if it doesn't feel as good as he expected? Or somehow it doesn't work?

"Just do it," I beg. "Please." I reach behind me and grab his hand. "I need you inside me." And it's true. I don't want it to be just Dad. It's wrong if Dominick's not here with me, step by step.

Dom's eyes flare at my words. I glance down and see that he's rock hard. Somewhere along the way he discarded his pants. I bend over, one hand on Dad's chest and the other bracing on the bed. I stick my ass out so that Dominick has the best access possible.

And then I feel him there. Nudging and exploratory at first. The last plug was large, but just by looking at him, I can tell that he's bigger.

"Do it," I cry out. "I need you inside me."

I expect him to shove it in. Part of me wants that. In spite of how he's prepared me, I can't deny there are still some lingering fears.

But I should have known, unlike Dad, Dominick would never risk hurting me.

"Relax and let me in, baby. Think about how good Dad is making you feel. How naughty it will feel to have both us inside you at the same time."

A shiver runs down my body at his words. I clench around Dad's dick and then relax. Dominick uses the opportunity and pushes the head of his cock past the ring of muscles at my anus. I gasp and clutch Daddy's chest at the intrusion.

"Fuck, Dominick, that's right, fuck your sister. We're going to use you, little girl. Use you up, so *goddamn hard*."

Dominick leans over my back, his forehead touching my spine as, inch by inch, he penetrates deeper. Daddy finally slows his pace and I suck in air and hold it in my lungs.

So.

Full.

"Look at our sweet girl," Daddy hisses. "So jammed full of dick." He reaches up and shoves his thumb in my mouth. "Suck it," he demands. "Suck it like you wish it was your brother's cock."

And I do. I suckle and lick at Daddy's thumb. He pulls it out and it makes a wet *pop* noise. He smears the wetness all over my face and I chase his thumb hungrily, tongue out, sucking even harder when he shoves it deep in my mouth again.

Both my sex and ass clench hard around their cocks. Simultaneously, they groan.

"So fucking beautiful, Sarah," Dominick mutters, one arm slipping around my waist from behind as he pushes in. I finally feel his hips snug against my backside. "I'm bottomed out in you," he chokes out. "Do you have any idea what this feels like? Holy shit, beautiful, I can't even—"

"Get moving. We're fucking a little slut, not spouting goddamned poetry," Dad growls, pulling out and then jamming back in as if to punctuate his words. So full of Dominick in my backside, I can't help an, "*oof,*" from escaping.

"Slower," Dominick snaps. "It'll feel best if we're together."

"Fine," Dad mutters. Then he reaches up and tweaks one of my nipples hard. I yelp and fight not to bat his hand away.

Dominick quickly distracts me by finally moving, a slow, languorous slide out and then back in again. Dad starts to move with him. They catch each other's rhythm and *holy God* it's like nothing I could have imagined.

They pull out and then jam in together and *ooooooooooh.*

Being speared with two cocks at the same time—the first couple plunges in, I lose my breath. It's just too much for any clear thought to penetrate.

But then Dominick whispers, "Touch yourself. I want to feel you come while I'm buried deep in your ass."

I don't have much presence of mind, but obeying Dominick when he says to touch myself? That's a no brainer. I reach down and start to circle my clit.

"Nasty fucking girl," Dad says when he sees me doing it, but he doesn't slow his pace, still matching Dominick. Both of them start to pick up speed. I can hear Dominick's balls slap my ass every time he plunges in.

Dad's long cock is hitting a spot so deep inside, right where the wall between his and Dominick's dicks gets compressed by the pressure of both of them stuffing me so full.

Oh God, just imagining the picture we make! Me sandwiched between these two huge, virile men, both of their cocks disappearing inside me. And the pleasure I'm bringing both of them. Dominick's told me he's dreamed of getting in my ass for weeks on end. And now he's there.

And Dad—*Daddy*—however screwed up he might be with liking to give pain, he also brings pleasure. Such pleasure, and in combination with Dominick, *oh God*, the two of them together—

I circle and press down hard on my clit—

Oh my God, they're fucking me so good. There's no other word for what they're doing. Fucking. *Fucking.*

My head thrashes back and forth and that's when I see us in the mirror over the bureau. There I am, riding Daddy. And Dominick, pumping into me furiously, his ass muscles flexing with every thrust—

It strikes like lightning.

"*Oh my God!*" I screech, rubbing myself even more furiously. I can't— *It's too—* I—

Light and heat and color—

I collapse on top of Daddy but continue to rub because, oh Jesus Christ, *it's still going.*

"Fuck, look at her getting off," one of them says, I can't even tell which one because I'm riding so high, pumping my hips and riding them as hard as they're riding me.

Their rhythm gets off, it feels like both of them are in a race to jam into me the fastest, ride me the hardest. I don't care because oh God, oh *fuck*, it's *still* going, I'm still riding it.

I rub and chase and more squeaks come out of my mouth as pleasure rolls through my stomach and then back down through my sex.

Arms wrap around me and someone squeezes my breasts. The surge ratchets even higher—like there's a crest even within the orgasm itself. I cry out as I ride the highest wave of my life.

Almost there. Oh God, *almost there.* One of the boys lets out a yell and stills inside me.

But in my ass, he's still thrusting.

Dominick.

I move back and forth against him and my furiously rubbing hand, digging harder and deeper into myself and ohhhhhhhhhhhhhh—

There it is. There it fucking is!

"Dominick!" I cry out his name and he clutches me back against him. He thrusts deep and then stills. Even through my peak, I feel him shuddering against me cum pulses deep into my ass.

And it's so beautiful.

I love him.

He's mine.

Forever.

Mine.

Perfect.

Love.

Forever.

"What the *fuck* are you doing to my daughter?"

The voice is so out of place, so unexpected, and me still catching my breath after the most amazing orgasm of my life, that I don't even register what's happening for several seconds.

Not until my mother stomps over to the bed and jerks at Dominick's arm to get him off of me. She's dressed in a fancy red party gown even though her hair is matted and stringy and she's obviously in rough shape.

Looking just as shocked as I feel, Dominick pulls off and out of me. He quickly grabs his pants from the floor to cover his nudity.

Which still leaves me straddling Dad.

"Get out of here!" I shriek at Mom, starting to move off Dad and reaching for the comforter. But Dad grabs my waist to keep me where I am.

When I look down at him in horror, he's just staring at my mom with a blasé expression. "What do you want, Diane? As you can see, we're busy. How did you even get in here?"

I cover my breasts with my arms, abandoning my attempt to get off Dad. He's got a death grip on my waist, and to my everlasting shame and embarrassment, he's still fully hard inside me.

I peek back at Mom. She was never Mother of the Year or anything, but holy crap, I never wanted her to see me having *sex*. I grab at the edge of the comforter and pull it up to cover myself even though I'm obviously still straddling Dad.

"Get your dick out of my daughter!" Mom yells.

Dad shrugs his shoulders. "Not until you tell me how you got in here."

"I'm your wife," she throws her hands up in the air. "When you weren't at the party I thought maybe you'd taken a room. I never expected you and your son to be having a threesome with your stepdaughter at the fucking Father-Daughter Dance, you sick fuck! I showed my ID at the front desk and they gave me a keycard to your room. Now let go of her."

Dad does let go of my waist and I scramble off the bed. I hurry to Dominick's side, wrapping the comforter around me as I go. Dominick has his trousers back on and puts an arm around me.

Dad, on the other hand, sits there, completely naked. He makes no move to cover himself at all even though his cock is still half-hard. He looks totally unperturbed at what's happening. "What do you want, Diane? Why are you really here?"

She glares at him, then over at me where I'm standing by Dominick. Then she looks back to Dad. "My card got rejected." She reaches in her purse and grabs her wallet. Opening it, she slides out one credit card. "Useless." She flings it at Dad. "Rejected." Another one goes flying at his face. "Less than worthless." Number three actually hits him in the chest.

Dad's square jaw tenses and his nostrils flare. "You're testing my patience, Diane. You've been abusing your allowance and I told you that I'd be putting a limit on your account if your spending continued to be out of control."

Mom scoffs and that's when I really look at her closely for the first time since she came in the door. It was obvious she's not well, but now I see just how much thinner she's gotten. She looks older, too. Maybe just because she doesn't have any makeup on. Well, other than some garish lipstick she applied at the last minute. When she opens her mouth to start on another rant, I can see it's all over her teeth.

Her eyes are red and she's got the withdrawal shakes. She's always unpredictable when she's like this. "You're the director of a fucking hospital. You're not running out of it anytime soon."

Dad stands up, all imposing six foot three of him. He towers over

Mom, apparently still impervious to the fact that he's naked. Mom barely looks him up and down once before crossing her arms over her chest defiantly.

"The reason I remain wealthy is that I don't throw my money away on coke parties in the Maldives."

Mom's eyes flare. "That was a relaxing spa vacation that I needed because everything has been so stressful at home lately."

"Stressful wasting your useless life away?" Dad says scathingly.

Mom's lips tighten and she steps into him, raising a finger to point at his chest. "Take the hold off my account or I'm telling her." Mom nods in my direction.

Whoa, wait. What?

Dad's eyes widen and he grabs her wrist in what looks like a bruising grasp.

"Dad," Dominick says at the same time I step forward. "What's she talking about?"

Mom just lifts an eyebrow in challenge.

"Don't shit where you eat, Diane," Dad says in a deadly whisper.

"Well I've got nothing to eat right now," Mom shoots back, "so what the fuck do I care?"

"Somebody tell me what she's talking about," I demand.

Everyone ignores me while Mom and Dad continue their stare-off.

Neither of them look like they're going to crack any time soon so I look over at Dominick. "Dom?" I ask, my voice trembling. "What's she talking about?"

As soon as I see his ashen face, I know it's something horrible.

"I didn't know at first, I swear," he whispers.

"Shut up, Dominick," Dad snaps.

I take a step back from him, immediately feeling like I'm going to lose my lunch. Oh my God. What is it? What aren't they telling me? "What didn't you know about?"

"Why do you think he really married me?" Mom asks, laughing

hysterically as she tries to yank away from Dad's grip on her arm. "It certainly wasn't for *my* sweet ass."

He jerks her roughly. "Stop it, Diane. If you ever want—"

"Fuck you!" She leans back and then spits in his face. "No man's ever gonna control me! I don't need any of this shit. I was doing just fine before you came into the picture."

She turns to me. "He saw your tight little ass at that party we went to last fall." She gestures toward the bed and then at Dominick. "He had this sick shit in mind from the get-go but he needed to *own* you first. So he fucking bought you from me."

"Shut up, bitch!" Dad yells.

And then he backhands Mom so hard that she's knocked to the ground.

I scream and cover my face.

"Dad!" Dominick rushes his father and pins him against the far wall of the hotel. "What the fuck are you thinking?"

As big as his dad is, Dominick's bulkier. He drags his dad over to the door, opens it, and shoves him out. "Get out of here, you bastard."

Dad looks back at me one time, then shrugs Dominick off. Without a word, he stomps off down the hallway. The door closes behind him.

Mom just starts laughing like she barely feels it as she sits up, reaching up for her bleeding lip. She's cackling like all of this is the funniest thing.

"He had such a hard-on for you." She looks up at me through her stringy hair. "I was used to men staring at you, but he had it *bad*. He needed to be able to stow you away at home so he could spank you and do his sick Daddy shit in secret, then go and still be respectable at his fancy job!" She leans over and spits a mixture of blood and mucus onto the hotel carpet.

I stare at her.

No. *Oh God, no.*

Let this just be another one of the screwed-up bullshit rants that she makes up when she's high.

But she's not high at the moment. She's in withdrawal. She always gets mean when she hasn't had a hit in a while.

Still, I look over to Dominick again, begging for him to contradict her.

But he looks over more pained, sick even. "I swear I didn't know." Then he looks at the floor. "Not in the beginning. At the wedding, all I knew was that you were beautiful and that I wanted you. And then, later, when I realized just how it was all a little too perfect and I confronted Dad about it, I'd already gotten to know you. And I just couldn't—" His tortured eyes come back up to meet mine. "I couldn't let you go. Sarah, you know I lo—"

"Don't," I cut him off, shaking my head. "Just don't." He obviously hears the dangerous edge to my voice. If he utters the phrase I think was on the edge of his tongue, with how I feel right now, I think I might just cut his balls off.

I look down at Mom where she's still sitting in a pathetic ball on the floor. She holds her arms out to me. "Help me up, baby."

"You sold me."

It's not a question. She said as much. For unlimited access to money and drugs. She only had a problem with it when her supply was cut off.

"He promised he wouldn't do anything you didn't want," she says. "Now come on, help Mommy up and we can go home and put all this behind us." She tries to get up by herself but falls back down on her ass again.

Wow.

"God, Sarah, let's go somewhere," Dominick says. "Just let me explain."

I scoff and shake my head at him.

Turns out I'm seeing a lot of things clearer now. "I'm just like the fucking frog."

"What?" Dominick's brows knitting in confusion.

"You know, the story of the frog cooking in the pot? If you put a frog in boiling hot water, he'll jump right out. But if you put him in cold water and then slowly heat it to boiling, he'll stay there and get slowly cooked through. You and..." I swallow the tears threatening to choke me. "*Paul* had me on a slow boil from the beginning. Starting at the wedding. And I was too fucking stupid to know to jump out of the pot. That you two intended on making a meal out of me the whole time."

"Christ, Sarah, no! That's not how it was. Just listen—"

When he takes a step forward, I back away and lift my hand. "Don't you dare come any closer." The threatening tears finally come, pouring down both cheeks. "I never want to see you or your abusive bastard of a father ever again. I'm getting restraining orders against both of you. If you come within 500 feet of me, I'll call the police. I'm staying somewhere else tonight. You and Paul better be gone by the time I get home from school tomorrow."

With that, I turn and leave him and my mother behind.

"Sarah!" he calls after me. "Please, Sarah!"

I ignore him and continue walking down the hall. Away from him. Away from my mother. Away from the last of my innocence.

THIRTEEN

One Year Later

LIFE WENT ON. For a few months, I didn't think it would. I finished the semester in a daze, somehow managing to pull off B's in most of my classes. God only knows how.

Then, not able to stand even being in the same city as Paul and Dominick, I transferred to Loyola University in Chicago so I'd never have occasion to even accidentally run into them. I also changed my major to women's studies.

After feeling numb for a few months, I got angry. I cut my long hair short, declared I was a feminist on my Facebook page, and read a lot of Gloria Steinem.

But I could only sustain the anger for so long and what was left after that was depression and confusion. And just an intense need to *understand*.

How did I let it all happen and not stop earlier to question what was going on? Was I so hungry for family and the need for people to want me that I just so blindly ignored all the red flags? And why did

Paul pick *me* out of all the women in Boston? Well obviously I was young and naïve and Paul saw a good target, but God. Was I that pathetic, like I had a giant sign on my forehead—I'm stupid and easy to manipulate?

And what about Dominick? Was he lying to me the whole time too?

I love you. I love you, Sarah. Christ, I love you so much. You're my first and my last.

If only I could get his voice out of my head. And the memory of how his hands felt when he caressed me. When he cupped my face and curled his warm body behind me in bed, holding me so close to him like I was his lifeline.

God, was any of it real?

After everything, the months and months, the complete decimation of my heart and the explosion of my whole life, that's the question that tortures me.

Which is completely fucking pathetic! shouts my new internal feminist. They used and abused you! They had you begging for cock like a dog on your hands and knees!

But not Dominick, another voice argues back. Sometimes he wouldn't even let me give him head, and the one time I did he wouldn't let me swallow. And he did everything possible to make sex all about pleasure, not pain—

But he sat right there and did nothing while his father all but raped you when he took your virginity! shouts the new, angry voice.

Not that I realized it or even knew how to vocalize that it was what was going on at the time. I thought because I eventually felt pleasure, that meant I wanted it. And I did get off so much of the time. With Dominick, every single time, often more than once.

God, it's still all such a confused mush in my head.

And now, here I am, back in the city where it all happened.

For Grandpa's funeral.

I think it's the only thing that could have brought me back here.

It's raining as I step out of the cab and hurry into the church—the same church where Mom married Paul. Sweat breaks out on my forehead as I enter the foyer.

Memories flash thick and heavy, one on top of another. Dominick offering his arm to me before the ceremony, shooting me that gorgeous smile of his. The sunlight through the stained window highlighting his golden hair.

My throat gets thick with threatening tears as I wrap my arms across my chest and then step into the central chapel.

Where the aisle stares me down.

But no, God, I can't, I just can't walk down it again. Not remembering how Paul stood at the end last time and my stupid, naïve fantasies of—

Instead, I stride down the back of the last pew and then hurry down the small walkway along the side wall. I think I would have turned and fled rather than walk that aisle again.

The church is packed, of course, and I have to dodge people, make my excuses, and arrange my face to one appropriate to that of a grieving granddaughter. All of it makes me want to scream.

God, why am I even here?

Because you're the good girl, Sarah.

Daddy's good little girl.

I squeeze my eyes shut against his voice that still intrudes in my head from time to time.

How long am I going to let him fuck up my life?

At least he won't be here today. I made sure to inform the estate attorney that if Paul attended, he'd be in violation of the restraining order I have out on him. I have no qualm on calling the cops on him in the middle of my grandfather's funeral service. Grandpa's dead, so what do I care about sullying the family name now?

Some legacy we've managed to build for ourselves. I'd be happy letting all of Boston society know what a monster stepdaddy dearest is.

I finally get to the front of the church and take my place beside Mom. Well, sort of beside her. I leave enough space for two people between us. She barely looks my way. She's dressed all in black, with a huge ostentatious hat and black veil covering her face. No doubt to cover the ravages of whatever binge she's been on lately.

She and Paul are still married.

Doesn't that just take the cake? But that's fine. They deserve each other.

I haven't spoken a word to her since that day.

It was the lawyer who called to tell me about Grandpa. And even then, the sadness I've felt has been more of a dull ache than what I imagine normal grief is like when losing a loved one. I always felt like just a business obligation to him. Maybe it would have been different if I was a boy, but as it was, I was just the offspring of his disgrace of a daughter and a lowlife. Tolerated, but never actively loved.

And that's fine.

It's all fine.

Being alone in the world isn't so bad.

It's better than being duped into living a lie.

AFTER THE FUNERAL, the whole crowd travels to the cemetery where we all watch on, umbrellas raised against the rain, as the pastor says a few more words and then they take Grandpa away to be buried.

I do my duty. I stand by Mom in the receiving line and accept the wealthy and privileged as they come by and relay their consolations. I bite back my disgust as my mother fawns over each and every one. Well, at least until she's asked for what seems to be the millionth time, "Where's your handsome husband at?"

"Oh, Paul is at a conference he couldn't get away from this weekend. He works *so* hard. Daddy was so proud of him." Then she clutched a hand to her chest. "But Paul did so wish he could be here today. He and I just miss Daddy so much." Cue the fake tears as she lifts a handkerchief underneath her veil.

That was my breaking point.

I pulled away from her and the woman taking her arm, pretending to comfort her with just as much of a bullshit, sugary tone as Mom.

The rain had stopped momentarily, but I pop my umbrella open as it starts again while I walk away from the group. My feet are sodden in the wet grass. I wore closed toe shoes, but they were still no match for the weather.

It's the beginning of June, so it's a warm rain. I kick off my shoes and step onto the wet grass, running my toes through the slick green blades. The further away from Grandpa's gathering I go, the quieter it gets.

This is much nicer. Just the fresh smell of the rain and the feel of the grass underfoot. And the white noise of the water droplets as they land on the umbrella overhead.

I wander the gravestones, traveling deeper into the cemetery where the headstones get older and more ornate. Betsy and Norm Milner, 1879-1957 and 1872-1957. Besides her name, all her gravestone says is, Beloved Wife, and his, Beloved Husband. For being born in the 1800's, they lived long lives. And then both died the same year. I wonder if it was like those couples you sometimes hear about, where they became so attuned to each other that they died within weeks of each other?

And it's stupid, so stupid, but standing there staring at Betsy and Norm's graves, I finally start to cry. I didn't cry when the lawyer called to tell me Grandpa died or once during the funeral or burial services.

But now, looking at this loving couple, so long gone...

I hunch over as the tears pour out of me. So hard that I'm soon sobbing. Doubled over like I am, I'm barely able to keep the umbrella over my head.

I cry for Grandpa and for what my mother is and what she never was. I cry for the whole last year and I cry about what Paul did to me and I cry over Dominick.

I cry and cry and cry.

And then, when I'm all cried out, I take a huge gulp of breath and stand back up.

The rain is pouring harder than ever.

But I still see him.

I gasp, the hand not holding the umbrella flying to my chest.

Dominick.

Not twenty feet away, only semi-hidden behind one of the huge cemetery oaks, is Dominick. He's staring straight at me and he takes a step when he sees me notice him. He doesn't have an umbrella and he's completely drenched.

I freeze and so does he.

Rain continues to fall, slicking his hair down against his forehead. It's longer than when I last saw him, almost in his eyes. Even through the thick sheets of rain, I can still see that he looks as heart-stoppingly gorgeous as ever.

But that was never their problem, was it? They used their looks to lure me in.

Without really thinking about it, I retreat a step.

Even from so far away, I see Dominick's shoulder's droop at my reaction. He looks down, his rain-soaked hair falling even further in his face. And then he turns around and starts to walk swiftly away.

For a second I watch him go.

His broad back retreats into the rain.

Further away.

Now I can barely see him now through the rain.

And then panic sets me into action.

I start running after him. After a few steps, it's clear my umbrella is too unwieldly, so I toss it aside. The heavy rain quickly soaks me, but I don't care. The only thing running in a loop through my brain is: *No. Don't go. Stop him.*

"Dominick!" I call out.

The rain is falling too hard for him to hear me, though, because he doesn't stop. His broad back stays slumped as he steps onto one of the paths that leads out of the cemetery. He's just walking, though, and I'm running.

I have such momentum built that when I finally catch up to him, I almost knock him over when I throw my arms around him from behind.

He stumbles forward and then swings around. His mouth drops open in shock and then he grabs me up into his arms, squeezing me so tight I can barely breathe for a moment.

I close my eyes and sink against him. I ignore the rain and I ignore all the realities that stand between us.

It's just Dominick.

Holding me.

Clutching my head to his chest and kissing my forehead, my hair, my face.

It's when he tries to go for my lips that I yank away, the old pain rearing up.

Because in spite of the spontaneous joy racing through my body at seeing him and feeling his touch, *oh God, his touch*—

But no, this is still the man that lied to me. Tricked me. Seduced me when I was just an innocent, naïve—

I rear back from him and then swing my palm at his face. It lands with a satisfying *smack*. And then again, with my other hand, I slap him. I raise my hand a third time and Dominick stands steadfast, like he's prepared to take it and anything else I might dish out.

It's too similar to the way he looked when his father took off his belt that time to beat his backside. Like he would just bear it because he felt he deserved it.

I drop my arm and just stare at him. I don't even know what to do now. I don't want to be someone who hurts the people I care about. And damn it. Dominick's not his father. And I do still have feelings for him, even after a year.

Dominick's eyebrows fall, looking as miserable as I feel.

"Please." Then he drops to his knees and bows, pressing his forehead to my stomach with his hands on the back of my thighs. "Please," he begs, sounding like I'm ripping his heart out.

The rain is finally slowing again and when Dominick's back starts to shake, I can't tell if he's crying or if all the emotions he's feeling are so intense, it's the only way his body is able to let them out. But it's obvious he's a man broken.

I've just been so hurt this past year and sure they were both playing me, I never stopped to think—

"Dom," I call out in an anguished cry, falling to my knees and grabbing him by his shoulders. His eyes are red and he's still shaking so hard he can barely speak. "Couldn't stand— You thinking that I was like him. And what he did— That last night with your mom and the other times he hurt you and I didn't stop it—" He breaks off, his eyes squeezing shut as he turns away from me. He stumbles to his feet, away from me. "I shouldn't have come. I'm sorry."

"Dominick." I go to him and grab his cheeks, forcing him to look at me. "Stop it."

He keeps his eyes stubbornly shut but I give him a little shake and he finally meets my gaze.

And oh God, there's *my* Dominick. His hazel eyes, stormy and tortured, but so familiar. "Where's your car?" I ask him.

Still shaking, he swallows and nods his head behind him. I drop my hands from his face, but only so I can take his hand. As soon as I do, his fingers interlock with mine and some of his quaking calms.

After we walk down the path a bit in silence, I see his black BMW parked at the curb. When we get there, I walk to the passenger side and wait. Dominick looks down at me, seeming a little dazed, like he can't believe I'm really here with him. He pulls his keys out of his pocket and unlocks the door, then opens it for me.

Still without a word, I slip inside, grimacing a little as my sodden dress makes a wet squelching noise against his leather interior. Dominick just stands there for a moment, staring down at me. "Get in," I say, then pull my door shut.

My words seem to galvanize him into action because he runs around the front of the car and jerks open the driver's side. I look straight ahead as he settles himself in his seat, but I can feel his heavy stare.

"Well don't just sit there," I say, trying to fight off my own nerves as I put my seatbelt on. I'm making this up as I go. "Take me to your apartment." But then my whole body freezes and I jerk my head towards him. "Unless you still live with *him*."

"No." He shakes his head vehemently back and forth. "I cut off all contact with the bastard."

I breathe out and look back out the front windshield, my heart calming back down again. "Good. Then take me to your house."

I can see him nodding out of my peripheral vision. Then he's got the key in the ignition and soon we're headed down the familiar streets where I grew up. I turn on the radio and smile when I find that he has it tuned to a local pop station. I got him listening to this top forty stuff. He always had classical music on before he met me. *Boring*, I used to tease him.

I lean back in the comfortable seat—well, as comfortable as I can be in a wet dress and the gillion unanswered questions running through my head—and close my eyes. I don't want to have it out while he's driving, though, and I am curious to see where he lives.

Turns out I don't have to wait long. The drive is short.

"I'm just five minutes from Boston General," he says, breaking the silence as we pull into a parking garage. "Thirty minutes if I walk."

I smile, looking over at him. He looks tense again and for the first time, maybe since there's not rain pelting us now, I see just how dark the circles under his eyes are. "You got one of the spots in the advanced residency program."

I reach out and put a hand on his forearm as he pulls into a spot and parks. He expels a long breath and looks down at his lap, closing his eyes at my touch. I feel his muscles flex and tighten underneath my fingers. His left hand reaches over and he hesitates, but then lays his hand on mine before looking back up at me. "I thought throwing myself into my work might help distract me from life without you."

I swallow, lost in the intensity of his hazel eyes. "Did it?"

He shakes his head. "Not for a single goddamned second."

My throat feels thick and I swallow again. I see goosebumps rise on his arm where his suitcoat has ridden up. He's got to be freezing. God knows how long he was standing in that rain with no umbrella.

"Come on." I undo my seatbelt. "Let's get you upstairs and into something dry."

I get out of the car and he joins me. I follow beside him as he walks toward the elevator. He grabs my hand this time. In spite of how chilled he must be, his hand is warm. I'm cold too and like always, he's the one warming me up.

"Your shoes." He looks down in dismay at my bare feet when he pushes the button for the elevator.

"Oh right. I kind of forgot them."

"Christ, you must be freezing." He drops my hand in favor of rubbing my arms up and down for friction. It feels so familiar, him wanting to take care of me. It hurts too though, because all those memories are so wrapped up with the lies he told.

"Dominick," I bat his hands away, "I'm fine. You don't have to take care of me."

"Oh." He pulls back, eyes cast down, like he thinks maybe I pushed him away because I didn't want his hands on me.

The elevator pings and I step on. "Which floor?"

He follows me on, running a hand through his hair that has just started to dry. "Tenth."

We're silent again during the elevator ride. I don't know about him, but I'm furiously trying *not* to think about another certain elevator trip—and then, thank God, we're at his floor. His apartment is just a few doors down. He unlocks it and leads the way inside.

I'm not sure what I was expecting. Something like the furniture he had when we all lived together? Instead, the apartment is an odd mishmash of styles. A bright Jackson Pollock-like painting full of all kinds of mad color splashes takes up almost one entire wall. On another wall is a framed Rosie the Riveter print. The furniture runs the gamut from a comfortable-looking overstuffed espresso colored couch with electric blue throw pillows to a black cubist loveseat to a beanbag in the corner.

I look over to Dominick, one eyebrow raised.

He shrugs, looking a little embarrassed. "I'm trying to figure out my own style. It's the first time I've ever lived on my own before." Then he hurries into the living room and starts straightening some magazines on the coffee table, piling up dirty plates, and grabbing up some discarded clothing and socks that are strewn around the room. "Sorry," he mutters. "Wasn't expecting company."

"It's fine." I put out a hand to stop him, but he just continues rushing around.

"One second," he says, dropping all the dirty dishes into the sink and disappearing into a back room with the laundry.

I bounce up and down on my toes, then rub at my elbow, feeling awkward now that I'm actually here.

God, what did I think we could actually accomplish by this? Yes, I still have feelings for him, but it doesn't change the past. With how badly I was hurt. The scars he and his father inflicted... I mean, he's the spitting image of Paul. Even if Dominick didn't— I mean there's just no way...is there? Every time I look at him, I'd be reminded of all that happened and—

"Here," Dominick comes back into the room, his soaked suit exchanged for soft sleep pants and one of his characteristic dark blue Henleys. "I thought you could get dry and change into this." He holds out a terrycloth robe and a towel for me.

I'm too busy staring at how the fabric of his shirt clings to his chest, outlining every one of his defined muscles. Well, now at least I know he wasn't so grief-stricken by my absence that he let himself go.

And just who else has been enjoying those muscles while I've been gone? It's a nasty thought and one that knifes me far deeper than I would like.

It's not like I haven't tried to move on from him. For a while I tried dating any guy who was game.

And failing miserably each time. I slept with three other men in the year since I last saw Dominick and they were all terrible.

I mean, they were perfectly nice lovers. They'd all been picked out by my new flock of feminist friends and were kind, respectful guys. They were all the same way in bed. So gentle and respectful that I wanted to scream at them to just grow some balls and *fuck me* already.

"How many women have you slept with since me?" I ask Dominick. Suddenly I have to know. Screw the rest of it. This is all that matters.

His mouth drops open and he just stares at me.

The fucking bastard. I advance on him, yank the stupid robe and towel out of his hand, and throw them on the floor. "How many?!"

"None!" he says, the line appearing between his eyebrows. "Christ, Sarah, I couldn't touch another woman. I'm in love with *you*."

For a second there's complete silence.

And then I jump him.

There's no other way to put it. I climb up his body, wrap my arms and legs around him, and devour his mouth with mine. There's just a millisecond of shocked hesitation before he wraps his hands underneath my ass.

Then he's got me shoved up against the wall. "Sarah," he breathes out, sounding like a parched man being given a drink for the first time in days. "Oh Christ, *Sarah*." And then he kisses me so deep, so hard, I forget everything except the touch and taste of him.

One hand caresses from my ass up the bottom of my thigh, then to my waist. He continues up to my breast which he palms and then squeezes. He lets out a low growl when he feels my nipple harden to a hard peak under his talented fingers.

I grab his hair roughly and jerk him away from my lips. "I need you inside me. My mouth, my cunt, my ass. I need you fucking everywhere." I see his eyes darken right before he smashes his lips back on mine.

And then we're moving as he carries me down the short hallway to where I assume is his bedroom. God, feeling the flex of his muscles as he lifts me so effortlessly is such a fucking turn on. My sex is engorged and soaked already.

I barely got wet with the other guys. They all had to use lube and I never even got close to orgasming with any of them.

And then, even as Dominick flips on a side lamp in his room to illuminate his huge king sized bed with a stately wooden headboard, I feel a rush of such shame I feel choked with it. He didn't sleep with any other women because he loves me. Obviously I can't say the same. What does that mean, now that I'm here, back with him?

Am I back with him? Is that what this is?

He kisses me deep as he dips down and deposits me on the bed, his body smoothly sliding on top of me.

And God, I don't want to think about what any of it means. I just want more of this. More of him. *All* of him.

Still, the sense of guilt is there shouting in the back of my head. All the while his beautiful hands are on me, making me feel *so* good. Just like they always did. It's like no time at all has passed. Dominick casts the same spell over me he always did.

But I was a slut.

I went out and seduced other boys just like *he* said I would.

Have you been flaunting that tight little ass and making the schoolboys' cocks hard now that you know how good dicks feel shoved up your nasty cunt?

I pull my dress off over my head and then undo my bra. Next off come my panties. Red ones. I cringe even while I know, somewhere in my head, that I bought the color defiantly. That the voice in my head is wrong and it's not a whore's color.

But all I feel right now is *wrong* and *bad* and *slut*.

I get on my hands and knees on the bed and stick my ass out, squeezing my eyes shut. "I need to be punished. I was a bad girl. I seduced other boys. Three of them. They had their cocks in my nasty cunt. Punish me."

I brace for the blows.

None come.

I look over my shoulder. Dominick's there, crouched on the bed beside me, looking down at me with wide eyes.

Oh God, is he disgusted by me? Does he not want me now? I fight the tears biting at my eyes. "Punish me," I beg. "I'll cry for you. Take my ass. You can have my ass." I scoot so that I'm nearer to him.

He looks down at what I'm offering and then back to my face. And damn them, the tears begin to leak out. No, they're not supposed to come until he starts punishing me. That way they'll be earned and he'll know he—

Dominick looks down at me and I see a look come over his face that he gets when he used to talk about his terminal patients—such utter compassion mixed with desolation. "What did we do to you, beautiful?"

Oh God, he's rejecting me. I'm offering up everything and it's still not good enough. I'm disgusting and he—

"Shhh," he pulls off his shirt and then lays down on the bed, immediately pulling me to him, skin to skin.

"Shhh," he whispers again. He settles me against him, my back to his chest, spooning me just like we used to. "You're beautiful and perfect just as you are. You don't need to be punished for anything."

I blink, glad I'm faced away from him. I feel like I'm coming out of a fog, steadied again now that he's holding me like this. And oh my God, I'm horrified at myself. Why did I just— How could I act like that again?

"Can I tell you a story?" Dominick continues before I can respond one way or another. "Once there was a boy who grew up with a really fucked-up Dad. This boy's father was very verbally abusive and would hit him occasionally too. The father was strict and happy to punish the son whenever he wasn't living up to the father's exacting standards. The father loved to manipulate people and he was very good at it. So the boy grew up with a very skewed perception of how the world worked."

I swallow hard even as his arms tighten around my middle. "And sex. The boy got a very warped perception of that too. After being introduced to it by an adult who should have known better, the father decided it could be just one more tool to control the son."

Oh, Dominick. All this time, I thought I was the only naïve one. But I wasn't. In some ways, Dominick was almost as inexperienced as me.

"So the son never got to have sex without the father being there," he continues, "in control and directing every session. Doling out punishment when he saw fit. It was all the son had ever known, even though he'd grown to be a man at this point, and should have long ago stood up to his father."

I tuck my arm around Dominick's where it lays over my waist. So much is becoming clear now.

"And then the boy met a girl. The most beautiful girl he'd ever seen, different from anyone he'd known before. But the father had already set a trap for her, determined to pull her into his manipulative, fucked-up games." Dominick's forehead presses against the back of my neck. "At the wedding all he said to me was, *she's beautiful and sweet, let's share.* Those were his exact words."

I shudder at them talking about me in such crass terms.

"I'm sorry, I'm so sorry." He presses kisses to the back of my neck, then holds me even closer. "I didn't realize then that I would be helping him do to you what he'd done to me—completely screw up your perception of what sex should be. Christ, you never even had a chance. We were fucking predators from the beginning. I didn't know you were a virgin. That you'd never— But Christ, it doesn't matter. I'm so sorry. It'll never make up for— I don't expect you to ever forgive me—"

"Stop." I twist around in his arms and kiss him to stop his self-recriminations. "Stop," I whisper again, pulling back. I breathe out, pressing my forehead to his. Finally, I feel like I know the truth. I think about every moment Dominick and I spent together. Getting to know him. Us learning each other's bodies. And how I saw him grow and even start standing up to his father by the end.

"I believe you." I lean my head back and laugh. "Oh God, I believe you." The weight that's been cinching my lungs all year long finally lifts and I take what feels like the first full breath in twelve months.

When I look back down at Dominick, he's staring at me like I'm nuts. I laugh a little more before kissing his nose, then his cheeks and finally his lips again.

He's still looking at me like I might be a crazy person, but I finally let him in on why I feel like I'm suddenly walking on air.

"It *was* real," I whisper, tearing up again. But this time with happy tears. Such fucking happy tears. "And that means... you..."

"Love you," he finishes for me, eyes fervent. "*I love you. Forever. Always.* Until you're a wrinkled old woman and I'm a little old man. No," he shakes his head. "Way beyond that. For eternity. Infinity."

I laugh and pull his face to mine. "I love you too." We kiss and we kiss and we kiss and we kiss.

But it's quickly not enough for me. My breast are crushed against his huge, muscled chest and I can feel his cock, hard and long in his soft cotton sleep pants. My legs slide open and I press against him.

He hisses out my name as I dry hump him. God, it drives me crazy being this close. I'd forgotten this feeling—how my stomach absolutely goes liquid with desire when I'm in his arms. This pulsating need to get closer, always closer.

"Get your goddamned pants off," I groan, shoving myself against him several more times. He laughs, since obviously he can't drop his drawers with me wrapped around him like this. Finally, I compromise, reaching to shove the elastic waistband of his pants down just enough to free that beautiful cock I've missed so much. I grab it confidently and give him a firm jerk up and down, which has him hissing through his teeth again.

I grin and look him in the eye while I continue stroking him. I'm definitely not the shy, naïve girl he first met. But from the way he's grinning at me, he's loving every bit of the new me. His cock flexes in my hand, sending my own sex spasming.

"Found a new toy you like?" he asks, his devilish grin still in place.

"You have no idea." I lick my lips. Then I drop down and lick just the crown of his cock, keeping eye contact the whole time.

He looks like he might swallow his tongue, his face gets so blissed out. "Fuck, *Sarah*." He collapses back onto his elbows.

I keep a firm hold on his giant cock so I can pump him up and down with my hand while licking all around the bulging head. When I finally give in and suction my mouth around him, he swears and collapses back onto the bed, but only for a second before he's propping himself up to watch me again.

I suck him in as far as I can take him and then I relax my throat muscles to swallow him further still. When it's not being forced on me, I find that I love the power of this position. I hum around him and his hands shoot to my hair. He doesn't hold me down, though, he just starts to caress me.

"So fucking beautiful. Christ, Sarah. I love you. I fucking love you."

And then he *does* apply pressure, but only because he's pulling me off of him. I lick his cock the whole way off and let go of him with a loud *pop*. And then he's lifting my body up the bed so that we're face to face. His lips devour mine as he rolls us over and pins me beneath him.

"I need inside you." His voice is a low, hungry growl, and the huge cock that was just down my throat bobs at my wet netherlips. "Can I?"

Always waiting for permission. Never taking without asking. This is the man I love. Our eyes lock again as I reach down and guide him inside. We both breathe out in pleasure when he enters me.

As turned on as I am, I'm tight and he feels it. I simply haven't had sex very often—three times in twelve months doesn't exactly make me well traveled down there.

He's slow in his rediscovery of me, and his face reflects his wonder at every moment. "Sarah." Even my name sounds like a song on his lips as he pushes in so slowly, so achingly slowly, filling me up bit by bit. I relax and let him in. I want to receive him greedily even though I know my body needs a moment to adjust. He's so large and I know it would kill him if he hurt me even a little bit.

Finally, *finally*, he's fully seated inside me. We rest there a second, me full of him, pelvises touching, his hazel eyes searching mine. With as turned on as I know he is, it's got to be killing him not to be pumping for friction now. But he stays still, concerned eyes watching me like he's trying to see if I'm feeling any discomfort at all.

"I love you so much, Dominick." I lean up and kiss him, which causes him to shift slightly inside me. It only feels good and makes my sex start to thrum with need. I pull back and hold his face. "Make love to me."

And he does. With an achingly slow glide out and then another gentle push in, he starts making love to me. The warm glow begins to build inside. Desperately, I wrap my legs around his waist and clutch him to me.

"Dominick," I cry out, feeling so vulnerable in this moment. But not afraid. Never afraid with him so close.

I think he feels it too because he starts shaking again like he was back at the cemetery. He kisses my lips, down my neck, to my breasts, then back up to my mouth. Until finally, he just holds me to him, thrusting in and out, faster now as we both seek release. I meet him with each plunge, clutching him by the back of his neck, feeling his corded muscles flex and seeing beads of sweat break out on his forehead.

His features knot into an expression that looks like a mixture of pleasure and pain and I imagine I look the same.

And *oh God*— It's rising higher, but harder too. Not just a mere wave this time. It's building like a tsunami. What is he doing to me? I didn't know it could even—

We lock eyes and clutch at each other for dear life.

And then SLAM—the blast of pleasure bowls me over. I scream and scrabble for a grip on his skin. He continues pumping into me, harder and rougher than before until he finally stills and pulses so hard, so full—

Everything is a blinding yellow-white light for *one heartbeat. Two. Three.*

A glimpse of heaven.

Dominick is with me there every second of the way.

And then I drop back down to earth.

Dominick's still here. Sweating and his chest pumping like a bellows as he gasps for breath. Then he's kissing me all over again and moving his cock in and out several more times as he groans my name. "Christ, Sarah, I love you so much. You're so beautiful. So perfect. I love you. Love you. Love you." Until his mutters are broken off by more kissing.

I laugh and wrap my arms around his waist. I hold him as tight as humanly possible. I'm never letting go.

All throughout that night we make love. Sometimes gentle, sometimes hard and rough, and then gentle again. I touch heaven more than once, and each time, Dominick's there with me.

And finally, I know for once and for all, I'll never be alone again.

Want to read an EXCLUSIVE, FREE novella, *Indecent: a Taboo Proposal*, that is available ONLY to my newsletter subscribers, along with news about upcoming releases, sales, exclusive giveaways, and more?

When Mia's boyfriend takes her out to her favorite restaurant on their six-year anniversary, she's expecting one kind of proposal. What she didn't expect was her boyfriend's longtime rival, Vaughn McBride, to show up and make a completely different sort of offer: all her boyfriend's debts will be wiped clear. The price?

One night with her.

Sign-up for Stasia's newsletter to grab your free copy of *Indecent*.

PLEASE VISIT: BIT.LY/INDECENTSTASIABLACK

ACKNOWLEDGMENTS

Lol, this is easy this time around because, since everything moved so fast with this one, there's just one woman who helped me bring this book to life. The fabulous and inestimable Aimee Bowyer!!! Thank you so much, beautiful lady! Your time and dedication to making authors' books more fabulous is insanely awesome. Thank you for helping me hyphens, commas, and reminding me to always make sure my characters are fully-realized and rounded. Ten thousand hugs!!!!!!!!! Um, seriously, the exclamation points could take up half the page and still not be enough.

Thank you also to Linda at Sassy, Savvy and Fabulous PR for also helping to get the word out about this book even though it was completely NOT on the schedule, lol. *mwah* Linda!

ALSO BY STASIA BLACK

Dark Contemporary Romances

Breaking Belles Series
Elegant Sins
Beautiful Lies
Opulent Obsession
Inherited Malice
Delicate Revenge
Lavish Corruption

Dark Mafia Series
Innocence
Awakening
Queen of the Underworld
Innocence Boxset (Ebook Boxset)

Beauty and the Rose Series
Beauty's Beast
Beauty and the Thorns
Beauty and the Rose
Billionaire's Captive (Ebook Boxset)

Love So Dark Duology
Cut So Deep
Break So Soft

Love So Dark (Ebook Boxset)

Stud Ranch Series

The Virgin and the Beast

Hunter

The Virgin Next Door

Taboo Series

Daddy's Sweet Girl

Hurt So Good

Taboo: a Dark Romance Boxset Collection (Ebook Boxset)

Freebie

Indecent: A Taboo Proposal

Sci-fi Romances

Marriage Raffle Series

Theirs To Protect

Theirs To Pleasure

Theirs To Wed

Theirs To Defy

Theirs To Ransom

Marriage Raffle Boxset (Ebook Boxset)

Draci Alien Series

My Alien's Obsession

My Alien's Baby

My Alien's Beast

FREEBIE

Their Honeymoon

ABOUT STASIA BLACK

STASIA BLACK grew up in Texas, recently spent a freezing five-year stint in Minnesota, and now is happily planted in sunny California, which she will never, ever leave.

She loves writing, reading, listening to podcasts, and has recently taken up biking after a twenty-year sabbatical (and has the bumps and bruises to prove it). She lives with her own personal cheerleader, aka, her handsome husband, and their teenage son. Wow. Typing that makes her feel old. And writing about herself in the third person makes her feel a little like a nutjob, but ahem! Where were we?

Stasia's drawn to romantic stories that don't take the easy way out. She wants to see beneath people's veneer and poke into their dark places, their twisted motives, and their deepest desires. Basically, she wants to create characters that make readers alternately laugh, cry ugly tears, want to toss their kindles across the room, and then declare they have a new FBB (forever book boyfriend).

Website: stasiablack.com
Facebook: facebook.com/StasiaBlackAuthor
Twitter: twitter.com/stasiawritesmut
Instagram: instagram.com/stasiablackauthor
Goodreads: goodreads.com/stasiablack
BookBub: bookbub.com/authors/stasia-black